NEVER
SAW YOU
Coming

NEVER
SAW YOU
Coming

KLS FUERTE

ISBN: (PB) 978-1-956094-66-4
ISBN: (HB) 978-1-956094-67-1
ISBN: (E-book) 978-1-956094-65-7

This is a work of fiction. Names, characters, places, and events in this book are the products of the author's imagination or used fictitiously. Any similarity to real persons, living or dead, events or places is entirely coincidental.

The Universal Breakthrough
15 West 38th Street
New York, NY, 10018, USA

press@theuniversalbreakthrough.com
www.theuniversalbreakthrough.com

Printed in the United State of America

CONTENTS

ACKNOWLEDGMENTS

I would like to say a special thank you to my mother, Elizabeth for her unconditional love in making my writing dream a reality from the start, and believing in me.

Thank you to my children, Sèverine and Sébastien, for their patience, their courage and the light they bring into my life everyday.

A special thank you to my amazing partner Marko, my pillar of love and strength, for his unreserved support to keep the dream alive.

I would also like to thank all my family and friends for being there with me along my writing journeys. I would like to especially thank Gaëlle, my talented friend, who totally understood the images and symbols I had in my mind, and perfectly drew and designed them as the covers.

Finally, a big thank you to Ian and all the team at The Universal Breakthrough. Thank you for being so kindly encouraging and positive about my writing.

HOW DID I GET THERE?

September 1993, my second year in England. Just qualified as a French and Italian teacher. Ready to work in green Surrey, charming England… At last, I'll have my real classes, my real students, and I'll plan some funky lessons to have fun. The year at St Ann's College in Cambridge had been the quietest of my student years! Nothing to compare with the vibrant Sorbonne in Paris where I had studied between 1988 and 1991. Cambridge was so small, so self-centred, and I suffocated from the lack of parties and fun. All were so serious and self-absorbed in their 'we are Cambridge students' attitudes. I was so bored.

Luckily, the teaching practice element of the course gave me the hands-on experience, challenge, and stimulation I had been used to in Paris. I loved teaching, being in front of students, and sharing French and Italian adventures with them. This was not easy in a country whose language is spoken by the rest of the world. 'Why do we have to learn French?' 'Because you've got the great Beatrice Martin as your teacher now!' I never said that, but the thought flashed in my mind a few times, especially as I ran out of convincing reasons at times for the bunch of reluctant 14-year-old children who seemed to know more than I do about what really mattered in life.

I remember one day when my class of 'terrible boys', aged 13, was unusually quiet whenever I turned my back to write on the board. Unable to figure out what was going on, I decided to stop writing to question them and asked, 'What is wrong with you today? Why are you so quiet?'

They looked at me giggling shyly, but very cheeky as teenage boys can be. Suddenly, Tommy, a little cute chubby boy with brown hair and freckles, put his hand up and said: 'Miss, Pacha said that your red knickers are really cute at the back of your skirt!'

'Ooh!' is the only sound I could just gasp, my eyes bulging out of my head. I was mortified. I dropped my board marker and grabbed the back of the skirt and to my horror, my fingers touched the zip of my beige linen skirt. It was down! I pulled it up straight and harshly, nearly pinched my skin, staring at my now hysterical class of terrible boys laughing their heads off.

Following that episode, they never caused any more trouble in class. Amazing what a pair of red knickers can do!

But how did I find myself here, in Surrey? The classical journey or so I've been told. The little French language assistant training in the UK for just one year. Well, that was the plan, but love got in between and messed up the one-year plan! The Central Bureau, working with the Sorbonne, sent me to Hampshire to work in two secondary schools as the French language assistant. One year contract, to improve my English, learn how languages are taught in England, then return to France to finish my studies and teach English in some tough French school where the government would send me after passing the prestigious but notoriously difficult CAPES teaching qualification. Of course, none of that happened.

I loved it here in Hampshire. Cycling to school every day, in the rain, in sunshine, in wind, in snow, and in hail, was amazing and so invigorating! No, not really. I was not as brave as my new friend from East Germany, Ingrid. I used to shove my hair under my Rastafarian leather cap, not wanting my delicate curls to frizz in the wind. My face used to be covered with a black scarf, and I used to wear two pairs of gloves to ride the bike I'd been assigned.

On my first day, meeting my landlord, Lee Banks, he showed me the house, my room, the kitchen, the front room, the garden, and then the garage. He walked inside and I felt obliged to follow him. This was really unusual to me. I had never been a lodger before, and I was in a new environment, maybe that was custom to show every room to the new guest, even the garage. The fact that I had no car to put in the garage was not an issue. 'Strange custom, why am I here?' I anxiously thought. Lee then walked towards a large silver sheet and pulled it off with a giant smile. His tall stature impressed me, he was obviously very sporty. 'There is your bike!' He announced so proudly and happy of his special uncovered surprise. 'But I didn't ask for any bike,' I asked perplexed. 'You have no choice, love, there is no public transport here. One bus a week to London.'

'One bus a week?' I screamed very alarmed. Lee was not joking, he did not try to explain anything more. I had to ride a bike and that was it. I learnt to love it, but it took me time. In the end, I felt independent and free with my new cheap transport.

Within a week in Hampshire, the shop keepers used to welcome me, saying, 'Hi, are you the French girl in town?' That would be without me opening my mouth, so they had not heard my French accent yet. I thought they were very perceptive of my French style with my bright orange duffle coat, my big scarf, and trendy boots. Then, a week later, I realised that in the village, I was the only black girl. The French girl was therefore very easily identified by the cute little community. Shame for my French style, they probably did not even notice it.

I flirted outrageously with John, the attractive PE teacher in school. John was tall and quite handsome, was curious about me, and invited me for a drink. I had nothing planned so I went along and met him in a pub after school. We chatted and he was quite interesting, sporty obviously, and also had good conversation. A few days later, at his flat, two minutes from mine, I discovered that he was a good kisser, a good dancer, but mad about rock and roll and Elvis, not really my tastes, but I went along for the fun of it. I was on a discovery journey of England. Our relationship lasted one month, September to October 1991. We stopped when he spent one evening crying over his ex-girlfriend he had left in Winchester. I more or less decided that he and I would not be a good match. We parted and remained friends. He offered a double cassette collection of rock and roll songs for my birthday. I was so pleased, but I never listened to it! Poor broken-hearted John ...

Meanwhile, Ingrid met Peter, a young French teacher at our school. He was a supply teacher—a very gifted man who could speak French, German, Spanish, and Italian; cute, but not for me. Peter was always impeccably smart, but never sexy or attractive in that way. He looked too studentish for me, and anyway, Ingrid seemed to be very mellow in his presence, so no room for me to flirt there.

One evening, Ingrid and Peter invited me to join them in a pub as Nicholas, Peter's brother, was in England for the weekend. What a brother he was! Nicholas came to pick us up with Peter and we were crowded in his dark blue Ford car that was very noisy indeed. When Peter introduced him, Nicholas said, 'Hello, guys!' His accent took me by surprise. He was English, but his voice was extremely nasal, and to me, he sounded Australian. Being in the back seat with Ingrid, I could not see his face straight away, but I could guess he was very attractive, and the long fingers he ran through his hair let me imagine he was tall. I was right.

As we left the car to enter the pub, Nicholas turned out to be a very intriguing guy to look at—ginger hair, bright clever green eyes, and a smile so wide—I could not resist feeling happy just looking at him. We sat, drank, and laughed for hours. I was immediately under his charm, and he was under mine, I could sense it. He loved my accent, the gap in my teeth, and my long black curls. He made no shy requests to see me again; there was no doubt we were attracted to each other. Nicholas was 23, I was just 21, it was Christmas time, and I felt the new year would be a very good one. He was a steward for British Airways and staying in the UK for just three days before his next flight.

We met every day after that first night, went dining, to the movies, or just stayed in drinking tea or coke. Nicholas could cook; he was a qualified chef and was indeed horrified when he tried to eat my extremely salty pasta. I was independent, but a hopeless cook. We laughed and joked a lot. We did so much together. Thanks to his job, he took me on board to fly to New York, Boston, LA, we even went skiing with his crew to Mammoth Mountain.

Nicholas was the reason I stayed in England for more than a year. When Cambridge University wrote to me to ask me for an interview to start a Teaching Training course to enable me to teach languages in the UK, with my fees paid by the European Union if I stayed for two years after, I had no hesitations. Nicholas and I had been together for eight months, and all was going well. We were even stupidly talking about mixed babies with ginger hair, intriguing, but made dreamy conversations for young people in love.

His posh family seemed to accept me, and his trip to Paris with me was a success when he met my mum, Marine. What could go wrong? I decided to stay and changed my plan. I was going to teach French in England, instead of English in France. At least in the UK, I would be able to choose my school.

Our summer trip to New York changed everything. Nicholas had been hassled by some guys whilst we were walking together and that really upset him. They had called him names I did not understand. On our first night in New York, I got drunk, out of control for the first time of my life. The giant margarita got hold of my brain big time. I was laughing at light bulbs and door knobs! Nicholas was embarrassed but was laughing at me, or with me, at the same time, I was too drunk to tell. There were stars on the ceiling smiling at me. I was so happy: New York, my beautiful flying boyfriend, and the stars on the ceiling. They were only real in my eyes.

We returned to England after a few days and Nicholas became distant, I could not explain why. We started to argue over what we wanted from the relationship. Our disputes did not last long, but still, they were more frequent. I went back to Paris for the rest of the summer and we caught up again in September, in Cambridge.

He would come to visit me and spend the day. I rented a room in a family in Comberton, a small Cambridge village with nothing but a huge village pond that I never really took time to appreciate. I would go back to Hampshire to spend the weekend with him and his family. We more or less recovered from the summer tension and went skiing with his friends at Christmas.

The journey lasted seven hours from LA to the mountain, but the warm chalet on arrival was a great reward. We became all mellow and tender towards each other again. On the last night, Whitney Houston was singing 'I will always love you'. So, I asked him, 'Will you?' He replied, 'I don't think so.'

My heart sank, pierced, bleeding, hurt, and burnt. I did not expect that response. I smiled, joked about his bluntness; he laughed, but we both knew that he meant what he had just said, so naturally, spontaneously.

In February 1993, Nicholas announced that he wanted a break, he was leaving me, alone in Cambridge. My world was ending after one year and a half of bliss. He did not give me any reasons, other than not being sure if our relationship was for him anymore.

I phoned home and told Mum I wanted to return to Paris. She said, 'No! You will finish what you have started. You already have a degree from the top Sorbonne university, and you are going to qualify from Cambridge University as a teacher. No, you finish it and stay in England!' My world ended a second time! I could not believe it. My lonely journey in Cambridge started. I pretended every day to be fine. Attended the lectures, completed the essays, worked on my Master's degree for the Sorbonne, which I had started when I became a language assistant the year before.

My world was so sad and grey, I did not notice the people on the course anymore. I became a ghost planning to become a teacher. He had left me after a year and a half of 'good sexy services' with no plausible explanations. How was I going to get over that? Returning to France was out of the question. I was stuck here in Cambridge, on a course I did not enjoy, in a town I did not appreciate, and with no close friends to cheer me up.

That's when I met Angela. She was French, but looked oriental. The truth is that she was from Laos, on her mother's side, and French on her father's side. We had met at the start of the course: she had come towards me and introduced herself as having some close family in French Guyana, and she was attracted to me as a French creole from Martinique. We shared the same boredom for St Ann's College, but hers was less prominent than mine as she was a resident on the campus and had made many English friends. My life at college had been a split between the family house and Nicholas' weekends.

Angela saw in me a friend in need, and I rapidly confided in her. She was a true angel with her jade green eyes, jet-black hair, and large smile. She used to make me laugh and told me how she did not think that Nicholas was for me, he was too soft and inactive for me. I used to protest, but in vain, she would not change her mind. Angela was very determined in her opinions.

On our way to London for our teaching practice, I discovered that she could tell fortune! Bingo, she was going to see when Nicholas and I would get back together. On the train between Cambridge and Liverpool Street, she read the cards to me using her Tarot of Marseille mystical cards. That was so exciting. I remember asking her time and time again if Nicholas was coming back. She would mix the cards, one way, another way, lay them horizontally, vertically, but every time, she would reply, 'No! He is not coming back!'

However, on one of our journeys, she announced the arrival of another man who was 'going to be extremely significant in my life. A very clever man, and hardworking too!'

'Nicholas?' I asked.

'No!' she shouted annoyed. 'Another man! And, you are going to meet him very soon.'

'Not interested, if it's not Nicholas.' I'd shrug my shoulders, turning away to the window whilst the train was swaying gently.

'Forget Nicholas, he is not coming back, I told you!' she would say softly but firmly, frowning those black eyebrows of hers very seriously and throwing a dark green look at me. Angela was very firm in her ideas, even more when they came from her revealing Tarot de Marseille.

1

The happy years ...

So, September 1993, my second year in England. Just qualified as a French and Italian teacher. Ready to work in green Surrey, charming England ...

September '93

Met Edward at school, love at first sight. A shiver went down my spine as he sat down in front of me in the staffroom. 'Am I looking at the man of my life?' It must have been the little round glasses and the square jawline. Or maybe, he is the man Angela had told me about. It must be him! I must be going crazy, fantasising over this guy who just sat in front of me. He could have sat anywhere else, but he came here, why? He is cute, but very badly dressed. That must be a sign: 'clever, hardworking' of course, no time for fashion!

One week later

I found out he was in charge of the arts and the school's productions. One day in the reprographic room, he appeared looking scruffy and absorbed in a script he was about to copy. I asked him if he needed help with the school plays, I could do the choreographies. He gladly accepted my offer and left. 'I'll get you, Mr Jones.' Mum always says that 'Beatrice gets what she wants.'

Two weeks later

After a long and boring faculty meeting, where we were both sitting opposite each other across some grey tables grouped together, he turned up in my classroom. I was alone at my desk marking. From the corner of my eyes, I had seen him coming down the stairs leading to my classroom. He came in and started to deliver his science about MAs in the most arrogant and obnoxious speech: 'Yeah, I've heard that you're writing an MA and it's really not a good idea during your first year of teaching!'

'What? You don't know me or anything about my MA. That's not your problem!' I became deeply furious and could barely control myself. Then he looked at me in a kind of cute way and said, 'You're quite dishy, aren't you?'

'What?' No idea of what he meant, I'd been living in the UK for a short time and had not mastered the slang language yet.

He then carried on with arguing with me: 'I'm telling you to give it up. I was writing a PhD during my first year of teaching and that was a catastrophe!' A little voice in me said, 'Did he say PhD? Brain cells do turn you on! Clever man, hardworking? Yes that must be him!' I smiled shyly back at him, but he had no idea why.

He then offered to help me with the MA, which I certainly did not refuse, that would help my plan. 'Okay, you can see it and tell me what you think; maybe you can correct my English spelling mistakes or verb tense errors.'

On the next day, as I saw him leaving school, he came to me to ask if Sunday at 01:00 p.m. was okay to meet at my house. Of course it was. He then rode his bike away. I was very pleased with myself: 'I'm going to have you, Mr Jones,' whispered the little voice in my head.

I could not explain why, but a new feeling of excitement was tingling in my stomach. Maybe Angela's words were gently throbbing through my thoughts and made me smile at angels I could not see.

Sunday came, and since he was coming at 01:00 p.m., I made some spaghetti Bolognese, just easy to cook. I had learnt that dish from Nicholas. For some reason, his name did not make me sigh in sadness, even though I had not forgotten him yet. Mr Edward Jones arrived on time and had a bottle of wine in his hand. We had lunch and chatted all afternoon. He was knowledgeable in so many topics and appeared genuinely interested in me.

He was so clever and well spoken. We talked about culture, politics, family, school, books, career, novels, food. Later that afternoon, he glanced at my MA dissertation, and since it was nearly finished, he had to admit that I was right to be annoyed with him on that day after the faculty meeting. He agreed to help me to finish writing it. I felt really happy I had impressed him.

October '93

We met in the computer room every day after school. I would dictate and he would type very fast, correcting my sentences as he wrote. That was so intellectually stimulating, and even sexy in a weird kind of way. I was physically attracted because of this guy's brain! Was I a total intellectual snob? I had been working on this dissertation for one year on my own and Edward gave me the opportunity to present my ideas and to be challenged. Our discussions about Afro-American writers' works and the African cultural heritage in their novels seemed to fascinate him. He knew very little about Afro-American literature and was really impressed with my writing and argument. From the intellectual language, we slowly moved to body language; one night he told me, 'I fancy you like mad.' Another night, he had flowers delivered in the computer room, could I resist that? Edward was so charming and kind, just what I needed.

I was still trying to get over Nicholas. Edward came at the right time and was so different. He was bright and we could discuss endlessly about everything. I was falling in love. He was caring, funny, and very intense in his discussions. Maybe because English was not my mother tongue, he felt he had to explain everything in great detail. He was such a chatter box, but a nice one. I enjoyed his vast knowledge of London architecture and nooks and crannies. He knew the history of every little minor street and building. He was fascinating! I was falling in love.

He invited me out a few times, and one day in Covent Garden, as I stopped on the balcony to listen to the music, some classical students played Carmen. Edward stood behind me and kissed me gently on the cheek. It surprised me, but I did not mind. I did not know what was to come, I was simply happy. We held hands and carried on enjoying the loving atmosphere of Covent Garden. The music was penetrating my body in waves of warm happiness, I could almost cry with joy.

After the loneliness of the summer term, and my 1001 questions about Nicholas' return, I was finally finding joy and maybe I was about to live a real love story, one that would last if I were lucky. I did believe in my lucky star, but recently, it had deserted me. Maybe it was on its way back. I was hopeful—a feeling I had not had for a long time.

November '93

We are an item, at last! Happy! First real kiss near the London Aquarium in London. We were walking when he suddenly stopped and pulled my hips towards him to kiss me passionately. It was cold and windy, but I felt warm inside. I closed my eyes and savoured his lips against mine. They were soft, we just merged.

When he released me, he took me to the building site of the Globe Theatre. There, we shouted out loud, like children, in the middle of the arena, it echoed. It was fun and sweet to feel careless and free.

On the way back from our London trip, on the train, I cuddled against his chest and daydreamed for a while. Time had stopped and we were both relaxing in each other's arms when I heard, 'Hi miss, hi sir!' We both looked up and saw the very familiar face of Anna, our 14-year-old cheeky student. Oh my God! There was no doubt about what she had seen, there was no doubt in her mind: we were a couple! And the grin of satisfaction on her face let us know that the whole world would be informed back at school on Monday.

We said 'hi' back to her, she left, and we stared at each other for a minute, not knowing what to say. Then, I shrugged my shoulders and said, 'Oh well, now they will all know, we'll just have to face the music, won't we?' Edward smiled and we went back to our cuddle position. The train took us home, to his flat by the river.

Monday morning in school was quite an eventful day. Students and colleagues looked at me with a smile and sparkly eyes which seem to say: 'We know your secret now!' There was no point hiding or lying when asked by the nosiest teachers: 'There's a rumour going round about you and Edward … Is that true?'

'Well ... Yes it's true, we got caught on the train by lovely Anna, press agent extraordinaire,' I replied to old Patrick, science teacher, tall and heavy like a bear, but very funny.

'How romantic, that's nice,' he said smiling and walked away to his duty in the playground.

The following weeks saw a kind of complicity installing between our students and us. Edward would send me little love notes in sealed envelopes via a student who would deliver it in the middle of my lesson: 'Miss, Mr Jones asked me to give you this,' the student would say very seriously. I would open the note, pinching my lips not to laugh, or not to scream. This was really exciting; I struggled at times to retain my composure in front of the class, or not to burst out laughing at Edward's naughtiness.

His scribbled notes said, 'Hey darling, what are you wearing underneath your skirt?' or 'I love you so much,' 'What time will you be home, so I can rush to take your clothes off?' and even 'You are the sunshine of my life.' Teaching became a very pleasant activity with little note breaks to cheer my day up. My responses were not less naughty: 'Red lace and suspenders,' even if that was not true, I knew the effect it would have on him! 'I've been told that I'm really sexy, would you like to find out some more?'

Edward was never tired of writing to me. His notes would fall out of my register, or I would find them in my staffroom tray. He sent poems I had never heard off; he wrote verses and notes filled with love and passion. I was overwhelmed, completely under his spell. One day, I found this note in my jacket pocket at break time, whilst I was on duty in the playground, I opened the folded paper with the familiar handwriting and read:

You are the moonlight of my life
I am lost without you.
I need to breathe you.
My life was dark before you.
Without you, I cry myself to sleep,
To sleep in your arms is all I need.
I need you.
You are the moonlight of my life

I could barely watch the playground as I read this. I was floating; my feet barely touched the rocky ground. I could not feel the air, I could not hear the noise the children were making. Could it be that Edward was really going to be the man of my life? True, I had had that vision, that deep sensation running up and down in my blood, the first time I saw him and when he sat in front in me in the staffroom, back in September. Months had gone by and his passion was not fading. But was that not unusual? I was happy, so happy.

September '94

I move in with Edward, overjoyed! We have been together for almost a year, we want the same things, and we understand each other. Well, I think we do, for now. His flat is simple, rented, and he shares it with 'cave man', his solitary flatmate who moved out three weeks after my arrival because we were too noisy making love. Poor cave man, at least he knew what sort of flat mates he needed, and that was not us.

We tried to make the boys' flat into a couple's flat. Many trips to Ikea together followed my arrival at our new home. Pots, pans, plants, utensils, matching crockery, pretty little things that couples do not need but feel an urge to buy, all these became part of my growing into a woman. I was no longer the lonely student in Cambridge, living a family-rented bedroom in the extension of the house, or the French girl riding a bike in the cold wind, towards her cold rented bedroom in Hampshire.

Edward and I were growing together into a loving couple with dreams and ambitions. He was 30, I was 23, and our age difference complemented our personalities. He was a real man, not a young lad in search of fun and lust. He was not Nicholas, and I no longer missed Nicholas. Edward was the man Angela had seen in the cards, that, I knew.

There is one cloud though: he shouts loudly when we argue and loses his temper over nothing. I only discovered this after moving in with him. He ruined many trips to Ikea by becoming this enraged creature who could no longer bear the sight of a pot, or bed sheet. He had to get out. Edward would become so unpleasant, rowdy, and argumentative with me, and loud in public, it would completely make me feel embarrassed, humiliated, and ashamed to be the centre of attention of strangers around us. Edward would argue about the number of useless assistants that were in the shop, or about the untidiness of the shelves, unable to find what he was looking for. There were too many people in the shop, and he could not stand it anymore, we had to leave. His temper would rise all of a sudden like an explosion out of his skull, and the only action I could take was argue back in public over the ridicule of his behaviour, or capitulate to avoid a public scene. I usually went for the second option and felt really unhappy. We would leave in sulky silence.

Back at home, Edward would calm down and say 'sorry'. We row, we make up, and we love each other. Every couple fights, do they not? Life goes on swaying between our blazing arguments and passionate love making to reconcile.

December '94

Edward takes me to Covent Garden! I have always adored its tranquil little streets and its cosy atmosphere. Covent Garden meant sweet joy to my Parisian love of inspiring walkways and pretty boutiques. 'The suitcase night,' funny and surprising! It's my birthday, and we're going out, I feel so gorgeous in my long orange coat and its soft brown fur collar. It is cold outside, but I know we are going to have a great evening out. I wonder what surprises he has in store for me. We arrive in Covent Garden, the market is still open, sparkling with Christmas lights and heaving with Carol singing. We pass a merchant selling leather bags and suitcases, they look so beautiful, I have to stop and look. Edward is increasingly annoyed, stroppy, I do not understand why his mood changes so quickly, but I really want that old-fashioned-looking leather suitcase that is just calling me so softly.

'Why do you want to buy a suitcase now? Tonight? In the middle of the night? We are going to a restaurant! Where are you going to put it?' He screamed at the top of his voice, but I did not care, I wanted 'my' suitcase, and I wanted it tonight.

'I'll carry it, don't worry!' I replied sniggering at his frowned face. I bought it, carried it to the restaurant, and smiled beautifully at the waiter who, in return, hid it for me in the entrance. What was all Edward's fuss about?

We are finishing a lovely salmon when he gives me a huge box and starts singing happy birthday. The waiter arrives with a fabulous shiny cake, I cannot believe all the trouble he went through, Edward is not an organised man. Now I see why he was so stressed about the suitcase. The whole restaurant joins in to sing happy birthday, I suddenly feel shy, all eyes on me, all voices singing out loud for me.

Edward urges me to open the box. I undo the black silk ribbon and gently open the box. The tissue paper inside is white and crisp, I unfold the sheets. Underneath, very neatly folded, I can see some black and gold sexy lingerie, I gently lift the straps, but not too high, the restaurant is watching me. It's a bodice, I just can't believe this, he is so proud, his eyes shine, he is all smile and says, 'Look underneath, there's more.'

I continue to lift the bodice and see a little box. My heart is starting to jump. I look at Edward, I look at the box, I look at Edward, I look at the box. I open it and gasp, 'Oh my God, it's a ring, an engagement ring!'

A V-shaped gold ring with little diamonds at the top. I barely have the time to gather my thoughts together, that he hustles me saying, 'So are you going to marry me, yes or no?' half-embarrassed, half-impatient. The restaurant goes quiet, no pressure.

'Yes, I will' and Edward jumps out of his seat shouting: 'She said yes!' They all clap. I am so happy!

That night, I forget about all our arguments, our bickering, and his bad temper. He actually loves me so much that he wants to marry me and spend the rest of his life with me. He cannot be that bad a man, can he?

We leave the restaurant under the tender eyes of waiters and customers, it's raining outside, but we do not care, we are engaged! I cuddled around his arm, holding my leather suitcase with my other hand, and we walked towards the tube station. Covent Garden has never been so romantic!

Days and weeks pass, and my pride grows bigger and bigger. I am actually going to be married, for real, and this feels like the little girl's dream coming true. The flowers, the big princess dress, the guests list, all the planning is underway, in the middle of teaching, preparing lessons, and attending parents' evenings. Parents even say, 'Congratulations, Miss Martin!' I show off my engagement ring to all, and if it is not noticed, I make sure my left hand floats high enough in the air to make my ring shine.

But, there are clouds above us: we do not argue less frequently. Edward is always stressed, never relaxes. He seems to become someone else at times. I do not recognise him. And the pattern repeats, repeats itself day after day. His voice scares me when he loses his temper, when he shouts. His lips become so tense, his whole face hardens, and his eyes throw darts at me. His body transforms into an agitated monster who screams and yells at me as though to eliminate all my faculties to defend myself.

One night, I rebelled, ran to the kitchen, grabbed a knife, and ran back to him with the knife up in the air, ready to hit him if he shouted at me again. He looked shocked staring at me in the frame of the bedroom door. I yelled at him, my voice was trembling with anger: 'Is that what is waiting for me being married with you? Don't shout at me ever again! Here's your fucking ring, I don't want it, I don't want to marry you! I hate you!' I screamed and threw the ring at his face, it rolled into the bedroom, under the bed. The wedding was off. I turned my back at him, the knife still in my hand, and left him alone in the room, maybe looking for the ring, I did not know, I did not want to know.

My whole body was shaking with rage. I walked the long dark tiled floor of the narrow corridor to the carpeted beige and cream lounge. One thought in my mind: I did not want to marry this monster anymore. I was not born to be treated like that. I expected respect and tender loving care, not a part-time Dr Jekyll and Mr Hyde.

From the lounge, I could hear Edward sobbing in the bedroom. I went back to him, slowly, still shaking, realising I had just held a knife against my fiancé.

When I entered the room, he was on the floor, his knees bent under his chin, crying like a child. I felt pity for him. He looked at me, his face softer, and a small smile was desperately trying to appear through his swollen lips. He'd bitten them and a little drop of blood could be seen in the corner of his bottom lip.

'I'm so sorry, Beatrice, I will never do that again, please forgive me. Please wear your ring, we are going to be married in August,' he begged me in a soft voice. I remained silent, just watched. In front of my eyes, the man I thought was my everything had threatened me verbally with his swearing, shouting, yelling, screaming for months. Now, he was crying like a child, begging for my forgiveness.

'I don't know Edward, I need to go away from you to think. I will go to Martinique for Christmas with my family. Don't call me, don't contact me. When I return, I will tell you where I am at.' Those were the only words I could say. That night, we slept away from each other: I slept in the bedroom, he slept in the office, on the futon. The Christmas holidays were starting in two days.

I left for Martinique that holiday to return to my roots. I had not celebrated Christmas in Martinique for twelve years, I was anxious to join the 'Chanté Nwel', would I know all the words of my childhood Christmas carols?

Christmas in Martinique was magical and hot! My grandmother made it so special, and all aunties and cousins came and joined in the festivities. I rediscovered the Christmas smoked ham, the 'christophine' and so many other flavours I had forgotten, stuck in my Western European way of life.

I spent New Year's Eve on Anse à Prunes beach at 07:00 a.m. The calm sea had not been spoilt by any eager tourists, and I was the first one to dive into the warm turquoise water. I was at my happiest. Granny Anne's present for New Year: Anse à Prunes beach just for me! The tiny colourful fish came tickling my feet, and the shy sun bathed my face with love and joy. How could I stay away from home for so long? I promised myself to return home at least every two years from that day, must take care of my roots. Granny Anne was my rock, and talking to her about Edward and our difficulties, sitting on the warm morning sand, she simply asked: 'Do you love him?' I said: 'Yes, I do.'

'Then marry him, the rest will get better with time. You must give time to time. You are both young, you have a lot to learn about each other.' Those were her words of wisdom, without her knowing that I had felt so desperate one day, that I raised a knife against him. I was too ashamed and scared to tell her. What would she have said if I had told her that? I was never to know. Is silence always gold?

On the plane back from Paris to London, I had decided that if seeing Edward made my heart jump, I would continue my journey with him, but if I felt nothing upon seeing him, I would end the relationship. A very stupid pact with myself, but I was still too confused to make the right decision. The Caribbean break, maybe, had not been long enough.

As I left the customs section and walked into the arrival hall, I could see Edward's smile from a distance, my heart was beating really fast. He saw me and ran to me laughing.

He hugged me so hard, I could barely breathe. I was happy to see him, and yes I would marry him.

July '95

I picked up Edward from the Eurostar as he finally joined me in Paris. I had been there a few days before, to adjust my wedding dress.

Before going to my mum's, we stopped in a café in Montmartre, for a hot chocolate, cake, and a beer. Edward was fidgety, must be his nerves agitating him before the wedding. In our usual contrasting moods, I feel over the moon, we are getting married in a week! Actually, we were already married as we did the registry wedding in London in July. Angela had been my witness, and Paul, Edward's brother, had seen his groom outfit. Sue, his mother, was also present, but none of his friends, we were in a very intimate gathering. Marine, my mum, had not been able to join us, her hip operation had clashed with that particular weekend.

We had a fun night, though. My childhood friends, the dearest cousins Rika and Alessa, had landed on us early the evening before the wedding. They just rang the doorbell! I had no idea of their surprise plan and was in such a state of shock, I remained silent for five minutes. They came with Zouk music, champagne, loud laughter, and cheeky jokes about me as a teenager. They knew too much and did not shy to tell Edward of my mischievous young years out partying every night in the summer months!

The next day, the wedding had been fast and I had no pants on, and no bra on either. Mischievous I was, mischievous I will stay, even on my wedding day. Well, the underwear messed up my creamy, silky, close to the body dress, so I took them off. I told Edward afterwards; he thought that was the best!

In the Café de Paris, at the corner of the Republic avenue, in Montmartre, Edward was not drinking his beer, he was staring at me. 'Beatrice, I want to call the wedding off.'

'What? Why? Are you serious?' I asked half-panicked, half-joking.

'I am not a nice person and you should not marry me,' he said looking up and down with a ghost expression on his face.

'What do you mean, you are not nice? Yes you are. You simply have a temper issue, but we are working at it, you are seeing a counsellor, and we'll be fine. Darling, we can't call the wedding off, it's next week!' My voice was trembling not knowing if my words were enough to convince Edward that cancelling was a mistake.

What was he scared of? How could I announce that to my family, to all the guests, some were travelling from London to Paris? What reasons would I give? That he was not a 'nice person'? He did not make sense to me. I did not know what to do or think.

'I just want to do it later,' he added, still looking very strange, absent.

'But Edward, don't worry, we'll be fine. We cannot cancel now, it's too late. You are a nice guy, I know that, you just need to have more confidence in yourself,' I told him, trying to reassure him that we were making the right decision.

'Fine, you're right, I'm just being stupid, please forgive me.' He then got hold of my chin and kissed me tenderly on the lips. We left the café and its chatting crowd. We walked home to my mother's house, in silence. We never spoke about that again. I never mentioned a word to my family.

August '95

The big day in the suburb of Paris, in my home town, Argenteuil. We had sixty guests from Paris and from London. A very small and intimate wedding, full of fun and joy. I arrived late, of course, but in a 1950s Citroën, a big surprise gift from Mum that morning. My dress was a 1950s alter neck white silk top and a floating skirt with layers of lace. I fiddled with the silky cords hanging down in front of me, behind my red bouquet of roses. I looked stunning and glowing as I entered the little church with my uncle Jarvis who gave me away. The long white silky gloves and short little veil were truly the princess' touch accessories. Mendelssohn's wedding march was played on the organ by Monsieur Du Chant, my brother's old primary school music teacher.

The small crowd, my closest family and friends, the snugness of the little church on the square made this day so magical and special, we all seemed blessed in an invisible ray of happiness. Edward's smile was almost frozen on his face, he looked ecstatically beautiful and over-happy. He could not take his eyes off me, and I did not dislike that. I had rarely seen him so overjoyed.

As the day unfolded, with the ceremony, the champagne, the food, a strange feeling of anxiety got hold of me. For some inexplicable reason, I was expecting something to go wrong at any minute. I feared that his monster mood would surface at any moment—especially in the presence of his stepfather whom he hated.

Edward never appreciated Angus. He used to find him 'vulgar' for his tendency to belch in public and never apologising. Angus was an old war veteran with conservative and traditional views that totally clashed with Edward's socialist ideologies. When their political views collided at the dinner table, Edward would deliver a rosary of insults against Angus in the car on the way back home. He called him so many names: 'moron, fucking tory, tight arsehole', but he never said those names to his face. What angered Edward most was the place that Angus had in his mother's heart. He saw Angus as the man who pushed his father away from his mother. Edward hated Angus and all he represented. Would he be able to tolerate him on our wedding day without any issues? How long would he endure Angus' comments about the cost of our wedding, or the cost of the Eurostar and long car journey from Argenteuil to the village by the Seine? How long would Edward last without exploding on Angus?

I was looking at this newly-wed man wondering if he was really happy and committed to me. He had wanted to cancel the wedding. Had I made an enormous mistake? Was this day going to make him forget these negative thoughts about 'not being a nice person to marry me?' I dismissed my poor intuition when I heard 'Unchained Melody', and felt my husband's hands holding my hips to take me to the dance floor for our first wedding dance.

So, I married Edward Jones in France and became Beatrice Jones-Martin. We became the Jones-Martin. It was his idea to take my surname too, not just my heart. We continued to rent the flat in Belmont, by the park, and worked at the same school.

September '96

Promotion for me into Renaissance High School, inner city with school super head teacher, Bill Hutchins. Bill is really imposing when you first meet him, a very powerful and charismatic guy, with a huge smile, and he calls you 'my friend'. I went through a very unusual and informal interview with him and his deputy head, a large lady with a motherly touch about her. I accept the post of second in charge of languages. In spite of all the bad reputation of the school, it felt just right for me, a successful career move.

Renaissance High School is so challenging! The children can be total little monsters, but despite my struggling first weeks, I managed to find a way to earn their respect and teach them French and Italian.

Two weeks later

We buy our first flat in Putney. I am blindly happy, but is he? The flat is a beautiful ground floor maisonette. I bought it from the garden, without seeing inside. It was a sunny day in July when we were house hunting. Putney was halfway between our old school for Edward, and my new school in central London. The estate agent had been very clever, and I fell for it. Parking in front was easy and we entered via the garden door on the side. The flowering garden offered such a pretty view, it was irresistible, and so refreshing. Some honeysuckle perfumed the air and went straight to my dreamy soul. The birds were singing, I could not hear anything else. I just said, 'I want to live here.'

Edward looked at me with a warm smile and we followed the estate agent inside the property. I did not care, I had made up my mind already. The rooms inside were old and in serious need of decorating, but I could just close my eye and imagine the finished home.

Two months later, we moved in, I started my new job in central London, and a new life started. Our new neighbours were charming, all but the old lady above us. Grumpy, ugly, sad, and harsh, this old woman had nothing of Granny Anne's kindness. She complained about life all the time from the top of her kitchen balcony. We left her to her own unhappy devices and got on with our happy lives.

August '97

My husband and I travelled to Martinique together to meet the rest of my family and make love under the sun! Edward, the English man in the Caribbean, charmed every one he met. They loved his accent, his efforts to speak and joke in French. There was no doubt, he was accepted in my Creole clan and I simply felt proud to have found the man who would stay with me for the rest of my life.

We slept under Granny Anne's roof, and when the rain started falling on the corrugated iron roof, the sexy steam went up between us and we made love every night, as though there would be no tomorrow. We were hot, sweaty, steamy, and we were loving every second under the mosquito net. Two greedy bodies merged into each other with no limits for pleasure and touchy feeling hands. Edward knew every inch of my body and made me feel like the most desirable woman on earth. Martinique nights were so unforgettable.

31.08.97

We were back in London and I was doing a few ab exercises in front of the TV. After eating so much exotic food on holidays, my stomach needed some reshaping. My exercise was interrupted by a news flash: 'Lady Diana died in a car accident.' First, I thought I misunderstood, not having spoken in English and heard the news in English for a few weeks. So I listened more carefully, but the news was clear, LADY Di had died. I felt great sadness at this news. Tears rolled down my cheeks slowly when Edward entered the lounge.

05.09.97

Mother Teresa died—another news report which stunned me. Those two women I did not know, but I admired their generosity from a distance. What was going on with me? I was suddenly becoming so sensitive to the news.

12.09.97

My periods? When did I last have them? Suddenly, I thought about them, but I could not remember. That afternoon, I went to purchase a pregnancy test, just out of curiosity. My stomach was not getting leaner despite the gym, and my breasts were tender and strange. I arrived home early and took the test in the loo. Not really romantic to pee on a stick and wait, and wait, and wait. Oh gosh, the colour changed to pink in the two windows. What did that mean? Oh my GOD! I AM PREGNANT! Edward! How would I tell him? A feeling of joy and panic grew inside of me, like a warm wave about to crash on a shore. Edward came home one hour later. 'Darling, I have something to tell you, but you need to sit down,' I said calmly.

'What's wrong?' he asked with a worried look on his face.

'Well ...' I hesitated, 'I'm pregnant,' and watched his expression change.

'Oh really, are you sure? Please sit down,' he stood up in a flash and started turning round on the spot like a dog after his own tail.

'Edward, I'm pregnant, not ill!' I shouted laughing at the same time.

'I know, I know, this is wonderful!' He happily screamed lifting me up in the air from the chair to kiss me passionately.

Everything was going to be fine. We went out for dinner to celebrate, but he did not let me touch the wine.

15.09.97

I received a phone call from a man who claimed to be my father! The man who mixed his semen to my mother's egg, twenty-seven years earlier, had never been part of my life. Who was this man and what did he want? I had to meet him, but not alone, I met him with Edward.

He looked like me: had the same hands, the same lips, eyes, complexion, this was terrifying! Twenty-seven years of absence and the week I find out I am expecting my first baby, my father returns into my life.

A few days before, Lady Diana died, then Mother Teresa. I believed my baby would be a very eventful child. I gave this 'father' man such a challenging interview; the FBI and KGB would have appeared weak next to my interrogation techniques!

What did he expect after twenty-seven years of absence, tears of joy and opened arms? I noted down everything he said: his reasons for disappearing, his sheepish attempts to find me when I was 7, then 12, so he said. He 'followed' me and knew I had studied at The Sorbonne and was 'proud' of me! Unbelievable cheek! I was so angry that night, in front of that total stranger, whom I knew was my father, but I could not scream my fury out of my body; I was pregnant and had to stay calm. He wanted me to meet my 'brothers and sisters', he had had six children after me, and adopted one. They all had different mothers he had left behind. A serial bad father, that's who he was. What sort of future relationship could I possibly have with this person? I had no idea.

When we parted, Edward held me tight in his arms. He had tried to ask some questions in his struggling French. He had been there with me, and that was all I had needed. He had been there for me. We went home and left that man at Putney East station to return to his hotel. My father had been and gone, one night in my life.

04.04.98

Passed my driving test eight months pregnant! The most awful turn in the road ever attempted: the car stalled, the breaks screeched, and I could not see or think about what I was doing, I was so nervous. Convinced that I had failed the test, I nearly screamed as the inspector told me, 'You have passed your test, Madame.' I'm sure he was worried that I would start labour in the car if he had failed me.

10.05.98

Birth of Sylvie, our daughter, we are so happy. She is so beautiful, with black silky hair and deep dark eyes. Her lips were pale pink. When we first saw her, we both looked at each other, puzzled: 'She is all white!' We expected a cappuccino baby from our mixture, but no, she was white, just like 'Maman La' then, my great grandmother, in Martinique. She was so beautiful, I could not take my eyes away from her, my greatest achievement. We were so proud, so overwhelmed by that inexplicable feeling of love for our first child.

Soon after her birth, Edward left Surrey to teach in Hackney, but that was not a successful move. He spent three terms there and struggled every day. The school he described was shabby, the students all rude and lacked discipline, the management awful, unsupportive. His school journey was a nightmare. He made no friends in other colleagues, it was all 'make it or break it'.

Edward came home every night with horror stories about the day. He did not seem to make progress with his students—a total contrast with my success at Renaissance High School before I left for maternity leave.

Edward moved back to teach in Surrey and found success again! He was head-hunted to teach in a very good comprehensive school, in the middle of the countryside. A very middle class population, good results, lovely setting, had he at last found his dream school?

19.05.98

Interviewed at Renaissance High School for head of languages, with Sylvie in my arms breastfeeding ten minutes before in the waiting room! In the weeks preceding the interview, Bill kept calling me at home.

'So, when are you going to pop that baby out? You've passed your due date, woman! I can't change the interview date, you know! The governor can't make it any other day but May 19th! Come on!'

'Yes, Bill, I'll deliver on time, you know me, I always deliver! I'm doing my best!' And I would put the phone down laughing.

Success on the interview day! Had no idea of what I was talking about, but they gave me the job, which was all I wanted. Twenty minutes before the interview, I had breastfed Sylvie and changed her on Bill's desk! Well, there were no baby change facilities in the secondary school! What was I supposed to do? My mum laughed at my audacity but was not surprised. I got the job, even with a few blurry responses! I would return as head of languages faculty in September and embrace the bigger responsibilities for staff, students, and results.

October '00

We bought our first house, 'the dream house'. We rebuilt the house together. It was beautiful and loving, like us. Once again, it was a house I purchased without seeing!

We had been searching for houses for a while and had found quite a few which we liked. Unfortunately, after multiple surveys, they always revealed some structural problems. We lost so much money in those surveys. In the end, the stress was too much for me and I told Edward to give up. I had decided to stay put in the maisonette for another couple of years and we would manage fine. I had been brought up in a flat with no garden in Martinique, so I certainly could hang on here. Did he listen to me?

One lunchtime, in sunny July, three months earlier, whilst I was enjoying an end-of-term buffet with some friends, Michael and Alex, at home, the phone rang. It was an estate agent who within seconds informed me that 'the owner wanted to have the asking price and had rejected our offer'.

'Oh, really? Well, offer a little bit more then,' I said to the estate agent, and put the phone down.

My friends, looked at me astonished: 'Did you just make an offer on a house?' asked Michael.

'Yes, I did,' I replied, proud of myself.

'Where is it?' asked Alex.

'I don't know!' I said, lifting my eyebrows, shoulders, and the corners of my lips, laughing. 'Well, I gathered that if Edward made an offer on a house without telling me, he must know what he's doing!'

Fifteen minutes later, the estate agent called back and said, 'Mrs Jones-Martin, the owner has accepted your offer, congratulations!'

'Oh brilliant! Where is the house please?' I asked gently and genuinely interested after all.

'Hum, you don't know?' asked a suddenly very sheepish estate agent's voice. He even sounded embarrassed.

'Well it is between Chiswick and Hammersmith, Madame.'

'Oh thank you for letting me know,' and I put the phone down giggling at our totally absurd and surreal conversation.

Yes, I bought our second property without seeing it!

That evening, Edward took Sylvie and I to see it, but arriving nearby, I had to close my eyes.

When I opened them, I pleasantly discovered the Edwardian house we had seen months ago, opposite the property we had visited but did not like. This house was beautiful and, at the time, we thought too gorgeous for our teachers' budget. And now, there was a 'sold' sign on it, and it was ours!

I kissed Edward at the gate when the front door suddenly opened and an old lady asked us if we wanted to come in, she had recognised Edward.

Once inside, what a mess! What a dirty old house full of junk everywhere, but the beautiful Chatsworth floor tiles in the giant hallway enabled me to close my eyes once more and do the future vision trick. I could see it as our finished comfy home, and all was going to be alright. I was happy, Edward had finally found our dream house.

February '02

I'm appointed as senior leader at Caring High School, six months pregnant! Interviewed by Pearl, who had been deputy head teacher at Renaissance High School and had left one or two years ago. The world of teachers is so small. She looked well and very glad to see me. We talked briefly about Renaissance; she misses the staff back there. What will it be like to work again with Pearl? We never worked closely together at Renaissance, she did not manage my faculty then, but there, we will be in the same senior management team. Oh gosh, can I do that job?

To celebrate my new appointment, we went to London with Sylvie on the next day. It was a very cold day, but beautiful. We visited the Natural History Museum, had lunch in a French café in South Kensington, and spent time at the French bookshop. Sylvie loved the French bookshop, full of toys and videos for her to choose from. Edward was always delighted about my will to make sure that Sylvie was brought up bilingual. So far, we were doing very well. She would address her dad in English and address me in French, for the same things. At times, it was amusing to watch her, we were so proud of this little clever girl. Sylvie could read in French and in English, only age 4, my eventful child!

The walk back home early that evening was brisk as the air was even colder than in the morning. I decided to dare Sylvie to a race to the house. She took me on it, to my surprise. I walked as fast as I could, holding my bump but stretching my legs real fast. Sylvie won the race to the tree at the end of our road, I could not go any longer, I could not reach the front door. My bump would not let me. Once home, inside and warm, Edward made us some gorgeous hot chocolate and we all relaxed in front of the new French videos of 'Père Castor'. Sylvie was happy, so were we.

Later that night, I felt so tired; I could barely walk up the stairs to go to bed. I slept so badly, turning and twisting, agitated and uncomfortable. It was around 06:00 a.m. when I woke wanting to go to the loo along the corridor. My legs touched the small rug and I tried to stand up to walk away. An excruciating pain in the lower part of my bump agonised me so badly that I screamed as I could not stand up straight. It was a Sunday morning, Edward, alarmed, woke up worried as he saw me bent by the bed, holding my bump with both hands. If I tried to stand up, my stomach was going to tear open. I was in so much pain I could not understand. Everything was going so well. What was happening to me?

Edward escorted me to the toilet, but I was now feeling some tension in my stomach, something was very wrong. I had made it to the toilet, but I was totally unable to stand up straight to walk back to our room. Increasingly worried about me, Edward phoned the hospital; the midwife said I sounded like I was having some contractions.

Contractions? But this baby is due in April! Why now? No! I don't want a premature baby! I was so terrified, we had not anticipated those complications and it was much too early. We were not ready to have our second child yet. The anxiety grew in my throat and my heart as we arrived to the maternity ward. Edward had called Mercedes, our Spanish neighbour, to look after Sylvie whilst he took me to the hospital. Mercedes was also expecting her second child, we became closer friends. She was a real joy to have next door.

Once at the hospital, the maternity ward settled me in an emergency room. They placed so many electrodes on my bump. They revealed that yes, I had been having contractions and was going into premature labour at thirty-two weeks. It was much too early to have this baby, it had to stay in and grow inside of me! I was so worried and scared, I cried with nerves. I had to stay in hospital to be monitored. They had some strategies and all sorts of medication infiltrated on my stomach to stop the contractions and make the baby stay in. I stayed ten days in the hospital before being discharged. My maternity leave started on the spot. I had not even tidied my classroom before half-term, which was the following week. Everything just stopped, and all became just about me and my bump. Bill was not going to be pleased, but I had to rest not to repeat that scary episode. I had the distinct feeling as I returned home that my baby was not going to be a sporty baby if that had been the way it reacted to a February brisk walk!

10.04.02

Birth of our son, we named him Julien. Our family is now complete, over the moon.

Will life go on happy? Julien and Sylvie are growing, but so is Edward's depression. The first serious signs of not coping with the kids appear. Edward needs frequent breaks from us. He spends days in the garden, or nights at the theatre with his students' productions, or takes weekends away to do his marking. He improves later, but work takes over life and 'can't cope' is heard more often. Less time for fun? Less time for us?

A few months later, I embarked on my new job at Caring High School. It was a slow start to adapt then enjoyment and success followed. Whilst I am learning to be a senior leader, Edward's jealousy grows underground, but regularly escapes with sharp comments at me: 'Now that you are senior management team, don't talk to me like a senior manager!' But, I knew I was not, I was just talking, but he took everything the wrong way, like an attack on him. Shouldn't he be happy for my promotion? It did not feel that way.

Life goes on ... Denial? Edward's depression?

2

First touch with evil

12.04.04
10:00 p.m.

I came home late after watching 'The Last Temptation of Christ', a horrible film. So much blood, so much violence, it shook me and moved me with anger. I opened the front door and heard him talk, so I walked into the dining room, he was obviously not sleeping. There, I caught Edward masturbating in front of his laptop. He did not hear me. I just stood behind him, in the doorway watching him moaning with pleasure whilst looking at some vulgar girls' pictures on his screen.

I shouted, 'Edward, what are you doing?' He jumped out of his skin and tried to do his zip up rapidly, but there was no doubt on what I'd seen. 'I, I, nothing. Just, just …' No words could come out of his mouth.

'What are you watching? You're having a wank here while I'm out at the movie? You're watching porn? I'm not good enough for you?' My questions just fired at his face like a shotgun. He said nothing, stood up, and walked past me, without looking at me in the eyes, he went upstairs fast. I could feel his shame and embarrassment as he brushed past my arm in the doorway.

Edward looked enormously shameful, but how could he do that to me? My frame of mind was quite shocked and disgusted at once. I never thought that sexually, he was not happy with me. What could be turning him on more than me? I was too appalled to sleep next to him that night; I stayed downstairs puzzled, angry, sad, feeling like my husband was a disgusting man. Questions were troubling my mind: What was he looking at before I arrived? How could he? He had never said anything about porn? How long had he been looking at porn? What else was he hiding from me? So, I turned on his laptop whilst he was upstairs in bed.

In his inbox, I spotted lots of e-mails from a certain Ariana Mainyul: the name rang a bell. She was one of his students, a violinist, he had spoken about her talents a few times. But why was she writing to him so much and so late at night? So I opened one e-mail, found a whole paragraph from that Ariana Mainyul, who made some very personal comments about his professional career and his personality.

From: Ariana Mainyul
To: Edward
Sent: 12 March 2004, 10:44 p.m.
Subject: Reasons

I read the e-mails. I would really love to meet you face to face to chat about them. However, knowing you ... *[How much does she know Edward, what is this?]*, I imagine that you must have been so over the top, in a very melodramatic sort of way, which may have been too much for them to acknowledge—NEVER lose this fantastic quality!! *[This is beyond teacher student/teacher rapport! Why is this girl discussing Edward's failed interview with him? I never do that with my students!]* Believe that you have so much to offer and you have the energy to deliver it. You probably need to slow down and take a one thing at a time approach. Must be honest with you. I really want us *[she says 'us'?]* to spend some time collaborating ideas in our arts—could we sometime?*[She is asking my husband on a date?]*

Ariana
X
PS—sorry for the roxy thing—I thought it was hilarious (I mean, I know).

I read further and find more e-mails between them, I am gradually feeling sick. I know I am about to discover something very lugubrious. I am about to discover. I do not want to, but I have to continue reading.

From: Edward
To: Ariana Mainyul
Sent: 12 March 2004, 04:22 p.m.
Subject: Lady gets sexy!

Probably not a bad thing. My account with Yahoo is Edwardjonesmartin. The lady gets sexy joke—very funny (not!)—scared me to death. Thought your name had got added to some porno site!

E x

From: Ariana Mainyul
To: Edward
Sent: 12 March 2004, 03:15 p.m.
Subject: Lady gets sexy!

Just one more thing—have you set up another account with Yahoo? Cos I'm trying to add you to my friends list but am failing!

From: Edward
To: Ariana Mainyul
Sent: 11 March 2004, 08:44 p.m.
Subject: Test

Delete everything we send straight away after reading! Hanging on to anything in this relationship except our memories is very dangerous till after you leave sixth form, Ariana. *[Oh my God! Oh my God! No! No!]* There—said it—we have a relationship.
*[I can't believe what I'm reading, Edward is cheating on me with a stude*nt? No, no, that's not possible! Oh my God, what am I

going to do? My heart is pumping out through my chest … I'm sweating, panting. Oh no, God no!]

Have you been out with James yet? I'm sure you'll enjoy it. E x

From: Ariana Mainyul
To: Edward
Sent: 11 March 2004 08:41 p.m.

The test was successful—well done

From: Edward
To: Ariana Mainyul
Sent: 4 March 2004, 08:30 p.m.
Subject: Test

Hi there my love. Wished we had spoken last night. Did you like the film? *[What film? What fucking film? A porn film? I'm going to vomit!]* Now I want it back so bring it and I can watch it again!!!! *[Maybe not porn, but what film?]*

From: Edward
To: Ariana Mainyul
Sent: 10 March 2004, 02:14 p.m.
Subject: Easter break

And now for the bad news. It looks like Beatrice is not going away after all at Easter. So our plans to be together will be scuppered. *[I gasp for air, my heart is going stop, it's beating too fast, I'm sweating, I'm cold, my teeth shutter, I'm about to vomit!]*. I'm sure that we could always meet during the week. The Bank Holiday will be busy with the usual boring family gathering at my mother and step-father's house. E x

Crisis! My whole world has just collapsed, ended. I want to scream, but the sound remains stuck deep in my throat. I want to call out for help, but to whom? What do I do? It's late. I'm cold. My body is cold. My heart is hot. My hands are cold. My hands are hot. I don't know how I am. I'm lost.

Should I just pretend, like Emma Thompson in *Love Actually* when she discovers that her husband might be having an affair? I suddenly hate this film! Or should I confront him? I cannot keep this in; my blood is boiling out and will come out of my mouth. I cannot control the pulsations of my body. My chest is hurting so badly, I can't breathe. The panic attack is too great to be ignored. I can't ignore that, I just can't! I send her an e-mail.

From: Beatrice Jones-Martin
To: Ariana Mainyul
Sent: 12 April 2004, 11:23 p.m.
Subject: Your love e-mails with my husband

Now little girl, I have found your little love messages with my husband, you must contact me tomorrow morning to meet in Camden. If you fail to contact me by 08:30 a.m.

1) I inform your parents
2) I inform your head teacher
3) I sent them copies of your secret e-mails with my husband.

Mrs Beatrice Jones-Martin, the wife of your teacher.

I press 'Send'. I climb up the stairs with the fastest and loudest steps ever! I wake Edward up in a state of shock and confront him in bed:

'You fucking bastard! You fucking bastard! You're cheating on me with a student! You fucking bastard! Get up, get out of bed, we have to talk! You fucking bastard!'

God knows how angry and terrifying I must look. I drag him out of bed, down the stairs and to the kitchen, it's 11:36 p.m. He doesn't even look at me in the eyes and mumbles:

'It's nothing, we just talk ... and we kissed once.'

'When, when did it start? Who started? Where? How could you do that to me, Edward? How could you do that to us? What am I going to tell the children?'

I can't stop crying, yelling, talking, hitting him. My body temperature suddenly drops down and I start to shiver. Edward catches me in his arms as I'm about to faint with the shock. I give in anyway and fall on my knees; he can't help me. How could he do this? Why? He's got to go. It's over, I can't live with him anymore. He disgusts me: wanking in front of dirty pictures, cheating with a student, oh hell, what's going on?

Crisis, tears, and screams throughout that night. He begs me not to tell his head teacher, the girl is only 17. He would lose everything and would not be able to support the children. Depression at its best, total hopelessness. I give in.

'This is what you will do, but fail, and you and I, it's over! You will not have any more contact with her other than crossing her in the corridors.'

'I will change her class to the other performing arts teacher, they're taught at the same time' was his offer.

'No more contact, do you hear me, Edward? Or you will never see me or your children ever again!' That was the most painful sentence I've ever said to him and I really meant it.

13.04.04
07:00 a.m.

I cannot wait for her e-mail. I call her to tell her to meet me. She agrees then calls back and I tell her that I simply want to hear her version. She agrees and meets me in Café Deli in Camden 01:00 p.m.

13.04.04
12:50 p.m.

I walk past her standing at the door of WHSmith without saying a word, then I buy a notebook. Slowly from the back, I call her name, 'Ariana?' She turns round to face me. It's 01:00 p.m. She is short and really not attractive. I expected someone stunning and charismatic. Her big fishy brown eyes and her crooked nose are a real disappointment. She's wearing a pair of black trousers and a crop top, her navel is pierced, self-mutilation adept. She offers her hand for a shake, I ignore her. What does he see in her? My heart will come out of my chest any second now.

In the crowded café, we sit by the wall. My notebook on the table, I started to ask her some questions. She didn't even look intimidated. For heaven's sake, where is this kid coming from? She was very mature, articulate, and confident, but also very odd. She looked at me in the eyes, unashamed. Her thick black mascara line doesn't do anything for those big fishy bulging eyes; who taught her how to put make up on? And those tiny little fingers with hardly any nails on but covered in black nail varnish, such poor taste. She looks like one of the Adams family on a really bad day. The girl is so ugly! I am so beautiful and so confused.

'So I've heard Edward's version last night, now I need to hear yours, when did it start? How? Who made the first move? Why? Couldn't you leave and go home? You are meant to be this great and intelligent student, he is your teacher! What can you give him, your music and what else? How long do you think it's going to last? You have a drinking problem and he felt sorry for you. Get out of our lives! I never want to hear from you again. Haven't your parents taught you right from wrong? You are a disgrace to your family! What would your mother do in my situation?'

'She would try to save her marriage!'

I challenged her about the wet love message she left on Edward's mobile where she said to him: 'The only thing I am prepared to exchange for sex is my music and my violin.' She laughed, trying to minimise the meaning of the message. I was about to stick Edward's phone to her ear to make her listen to her own slutty message, but I changed my mind and kept his phone in my bag. Her explanation was feeble and did not make sense: 'She gets from her music and her violin as much pleasure as maybe compared to sex.' She really thinks I'm an idiot.

She said she was sorry, that there was nothing between them, just talking, but she admitted the kiss. 'Little slut' came out of my mouth; tears came out of her eyes. I did not believe in her tears, her eyes were dishonest. I told her to never see my husband again, that he had to change her class to Ms Misha. When I told her to go out with someone of her own age, such as James (as mentioned in Edward's e-mail), she laughed arrogantly! I kept repeating 'Get out of our lives! You disgust me,' trying to convince myself that she would get out of our lives. I left her in the café.

I phone her thirty-one minutes later and asks her if Edward had called her, she replies 'yes'.

'And what did you tell him?'

'I told him to leave me alone.' She hung up.

I started my car from the supermarket car park and drove home. I feel quite satisfied, I did not portray the weak and distressed wife. That Ariana is really ugly! What could he see in her? I could not understand. No charm, no nothing! She plays the violin and so what? What on earth was going on in Edward's mind? Is it a middle life crisis? 'I've just turned 41 and I don't want to die' kind of feeling, 'so I'll fantasise on a young girl'? If he is so anxious about growing old and losing himself, why doesn't he talk to me? He did not need to hurt me so much, with a 17-year-old ugly slut, for heaven's sake. You want to hurt me, choose someone more attractive than me. That one isn't worth the pain ...

13.04.04
02:30 p.m.

Return home. Edward knows where I have been. He tells me so. I ask him about his conversation with her and he reports that she found me 'horrible, that I doubted her music' and that he should not have told me that she had a drinking problem!

'Oh she did not like that!' he added. So she had lied to me, she had never told him to leave her alone. What was next? Saving our marriage? Agreement with Edward that he would change her class, and he would no longer have any contact with her? Deep in my heart, I was frightened that I was just at the beginning of finding out what he had meant when he told me before our wedding that he was 'not a nice person'.

3

We are in love again

Some time between April and June 2004

Edward and I tried to be in love again. We make love like there is no tomorrow, every night. He now calls me 'sex addict woman'. There is this urge that I have to give myself to him, probably in a desperate need to keep him as mine, to reassure myself that he still belongs to me, physically, emotionally, and sexually. Deep down, I wonder if Edward is a new man, a man that I do not recognise. I wonder if I really want to do that, like that? Our love making relationship is changing. He is more powerful, more dominating. I enjoy it, but at times, I do not feel that we are making love. He is making love at me as though he had something to prove to me, or to himself. What exactly? I cannot work it out.

We are now going out a lot. We are making more time for each other. I try to spend less time with my laptop at night and have less late chats with Pearl, but I miss our good laughs lately. Still, I was happy again, I thought. I would still pick up his mobile to run through his messages and recent calls. Nothing. I did not contact Ariana again after the meeting in the café. Edward and I try to talk about the affair, for I need to know what they were doing together, how they met, when, where. At times, he would answer my questions, at other times, he would become heated and stop talking. A shadow is cast upon us, will it ever go away?

A special weekend in June

I leave Edward to go to Fabiola and Cedric's wedding in France the next day. We call each other a lot before and during the wedding. I'm happy to hear him so often, he even asked if I'm being chatted up by some good-looking French guys. I said, 'No, I'm a married woman.'

I return home in the morning and give him a big hug in the street as I met him trying to walk Julien to sleep in his buggy.

4

We were doing okay

Mid-June

Edward loses his mobile phone and is frantic about it. This raises my suspicion. There must be something on the phone that I should not see, something that I should not hear. I fear that the slut is resurfacing. Edward probably lied about changing her class. He is still having some contact with her, I'm sure. Paranoia settles in my mind, and my mistrust grows. I can sense that the worse is yet to emerge. Happiness is just an illusion.

Wednesday
16.06.04

In the morning in the car, we argue about going to my head teacher's, Mr John, for his retirement meal. He doesn't want to come and yells some really hurtful things at me: 'Don't want to be there, with everybody watching me, all those SMT having a laugh at me!'

'Edward, this is not a dinner about you, it's about John! You always have to mess up my plans! All I wanted was spending some time out with you.'

'Well, I don't suck up to my head like you!'

Those were his last words before dropping me at school! I was so hurt! How could he say such vile words? He rings during the day to apologise. He insults, he apologises, he insults, he apologises … Dr Jekyll and Mr Hyde; this was whom I married. I needed to repair that enormous error. The voice saying 'I'm not a nice person' kept throbbing in my head. And I replied, 'No,

Edward, you really are not. I agree with you now,' but he could not hear me. The words were isolated in my troubled, anxious mind.

Juanita babysat in the evening so Edward and I went out for his birthday. While he was paying at the petrol station, I found his mobile under his seat. I looked at the screen, it said two messages. Naively, I showed him the phone through the windscreen. He jumped, he ran, he flew to snatch if off my hands! Argument follows:

'You are still seeing her! Who left the messages?'

He replied with a stutter, 'T-Tom.'

'You're lying! It was her! Why can't I see this phone? What is the secret on it? If you do not have anything to hide, then why snatch it off my hands?'

'Because you do not trust me!'

'If you have nothing to hide, show me and I'll trust you.'

He came out of the car and in a rage threw the phone in the street bin shouting, 'There, gone, I hate the flipping thing anyway!' His face was so hard, his jaws so tense, he was throwing darts at me with his green, piercing eyes. His breathing was loud and fast, felt threatening. I looked down to hide my fear and clenched my fingers together on my lap. We drove back home cold. Happy birthday, Edward!

Thursday
17.06.04

I phone Tom to ask, 'Did you send a message recently to Edward? Well he's lost his phone, just to let you know!'

Tom replies, 'No, I haven't.'

Edward had lied. I phoned Orange to pretend that our daughter had used our phone but they could not give me any phone call records as the phone is registered under Edward's name.

I return home hurt, sad, angry, tired. Edward phones me to tell me he will be late. Our conversation is short and cold.

He arrives home at 06:00 p.m. I tell him, 'I spoke to her, she said that you are still seeing each other.'

'When? When did you speak to her?' was his response. How illuminating! He had to check the time we were meant to have spoken, incredible liar! He had just been with her, so she could not have spoken to me! I felt sick in the stomach!

We argued nearly all night; for the first time, Sylvie did not manage to keep us quiet by telling us 'Will you two be quiet!' That was so upsetting! Juanita was out.

He prepared a leaving bag and put it in the boot. In the night, Edward left the house and called me from phone boxes in Hertfordshire. He was sorry, asked for my forgiveness. He spent the night out.

He was saying: 'Do you know how close I am to killing myself over this? Do you know how much I love you?' He worried me, but I did not believe him; we talked and talked. He asked me: 'On a scale of 1 to 10, how much do you want me back?' I said '11'. He returns home very late in the night. I'm happy for a few hours.

Saturday
19.06.04

In the morning, I beg him to tell me the truth. 'Ask me to forgive you, Edward,' and he does. 'So you are still in touch with her!'

'Yes, but we only talk.'

'About what?'

'About arts, about music. She is helping me to get ideas to develop music in my new school because she knows so many people. She is such an extraordinary musician who also has a love for theatre, this is so unusual.'

As he talks about her, a sparkle lights up in his eyes, I did not miss it! He is in love with that girl, he has feelings for her. Oh God, what am I to do? Why? I tried so hard!

Late that night, I cried myself to sleep. So it will never end! Even when you change schools, Edward! In the early hours of Sunday morning, I had a wakeup call and told him:

'We can't live together anymore because I cannot trust you. You can live here, but I'm no longer your wife. What's really going on? This girl is in your head? She is in your head and I can't share you with anyone else. I did not marry you for that.'

We argue on and off. He comes and goes out of the house. Late afternoon, he returns home happy and decides to drag us all to a restaurant. Maybe that was one of her genius ideas? We are cold. Returned home, what a mess. I feel so low, just cannot believe this man. Whenever I ask, 'Did you sleep with her? Did you have sex with her?' he replies 'no' but his eyes say 'yes'. I cannot believe him, I know there is more to it. We try to talk about it, but it always ends up in an argument. It seems that we are all so close to the end of our marriage. The air is heavy with a strange feeling that I cannot describe.

I phone John and tell him that the kids are ill so we can't come to his retirement dinner tonight. It felt so bad.

5

The last afternoon

Sunday
20.06.04

That Sunday morning, we took the children to the park by the river, to play with the kite, and Sylvie learnt to ride her bike without the stabilisers! We were happy for a few hours. We had a picnic and I asked him again: 'Did you sleep with her? Did you have sex with her?'

He replied 'no' but his eyes said 'yes'. He kissed me. 'Do you believe me now?'

'Yes,' but my eyes said 'no'. We walked, he held my hand. I knew he was lying, but I could not prove it.

Later, in the afternoon, he went up for a nap, he felt ill, was shivering, and had a temperature. He slept. An inner feeling took over me and I left him upstairs to search through his bag. What was I looking for? Proof? My hands had a slight tremor as I was rummaging through his black school bag. There I found a brown envelop sealed with no name on it, so I opened it. I recognised Edward's handwriting. It read:

'My sweet Ariana,

Well, I am overjoyed that we got to the rings stage! I should have never attracted you into this maze of troubles. I am deeply sorry Ariana. I wish I could lie to you, but I cannot. I am desperately in love with you my sweet Ariana. Yet I can sense that your emotions are in turmoil - it was the disastrous

attempt to make love in the field last week. If only… I know
that you have feelings for me, I can feel them all over your
tender body. I will never forget the light and joy you brought
into my life. Thank you. Ariana,

Edward'

My body loses control once more. The shock of this letter made my heart race and pulsate so fast. I shake, I go cold, and my teeth start to tremble. My stomach hurts. I want to vomit. I also find a TES page with her photo playing the violin. She autographed it for him: 'To Edward, with love always, from Ariana Mainyul'. I place the letter and the newspaper page somewhere safe in my bag. I feel so sick in the guts.

I am violently shaking with heartache. April all over again … I go up the stairs to our bedroom, he is in bed, sleeping. I wake him up with a shake: 'You love that girl! You love that girl!' softly I said in tears.

'What? You've changed your mind again!' he jumped out of bed.

'I found the letter you wrote to her. So you tried to make love in the field! When? When? You lied to me? Oh no, I did not have sex! You're a liar! Get out! Get out! I never want to see you again. Go to her!' And I start to push him around the room, all he could say was 'Oh no! No! No! No!' What else could he say anyway …?

He goes down the stairs and I follow him still shouting. He sits on the little chair in the lounge and I hit him on his chest, he says nothing, hopelessness in his eyes!

'How convenient to have your mistress at school and your wife and family at home. You have made your choice! You have chosen her, jeopardised everything we've got for a 17-year-old! You make me sick! Get out of our lives. You'll never see us again! You are nothing, you are less than nothing!' He was trying to put his shoes on and as I could no longer stand the sight of him in front of my eyes, I grabbed his shoes, threw them outside the window to hurry him out. On his way out, he looked at me threateningly and said in his cold deep voice, 'I need the car keys.' I refused to hand them to him; we struggled for a second, then he clutched my wrist to snatch them off me and left the house.

I sat down at the bottom of the staircase and cried for two minutes when a sudden rage took over my soul and made me call the little slut! Oh heaven knows how mad and desperate I was! I phoned her and told her that I had kicked him out. I cried through the words but I was also so angry and completely irrational! I could feel my desperation eating me. She put the phone down on me. I called back shouting at her, 'Don't put the phone down on me again, you liar, you little slut, when was the day of the field love making, when was it?' She laughed and started saying, Sniggering: 'I will not be victimised or bullied or threatened.' She did not answer my questions, she was laughing nastily. It sounded as though a friend was near her. She was really enjoying my pain!

'You have destroyed my life, you have destroyed my marriage and you will pay for it! I had warned you to get out of our lives and you didn't!'

My whole body was trembling; had she been in front of me, I would have jumped at her neck! While I was throwing a river of insults at her, she continued saying, 'I will not be victimised or bullied or threatened.'

I even asked her to stop saying that like a stupid parrot, I asked her if she had already seen a solicitor who had told her to continually repeat those words.

I asked her if she had heard of the boy who had been stabbed in the news this week. She said, 'Why are you telling me this?' She probably thought that I was going crazy by then. I told her that I used to teach him and that I wished it was her who had died! She laughed again and said, 'I'm recording this call for the police!'

That surprised me and I stopped shouting.

'Fine, and I'll tell the police what you've done to my life, how wrong you have been, all I have are my words, I'm a desperate wife who's lost everything because of you! You and Edward have turned me into a monster with all your lies, you make a very good pair!' I put the phone down, I felt so dirty and hopeless. Gosh, the words I used! It's all over now, must get on. I phoned Jane to tell her that I had just kicked her brother out. She listened carefully and sounded so sorry for the whole mess. She tried to keep me calm.

Late that night, Juanita returned and I told her everything in the kitchen at midnight. I cried and she comforted me. There she revealed how on the night I was at Fabiola's wedding, Edward had insisted all night for her to babysit and how he left the house really late. She was surprised for she knew that he did not have any friends, but she did not think twice. He was with the slut that night while I was at my friend's wedding, a last-minute decision I had made to go alone to try and save money. He had rang me all evening to check if I was being chatted up by some French guys but he had also spent the night with her. How sickening this picture was. I had been so naive, so stupid. Some weeks later, our phone bill showed me that on that night he had also phoned the Holiday Express Inn in Colliers Wood! A room for Ariana and Edward. How romantic! How dirty! I called the hotel to find out but they never checked in that night.

6

Love me so dearly / Down to hell

Monday
21.06.04

Woke up early, a lot on today to reorganise my new life. Went out to Chiswick to rent a car, a cute red Nissan Micra.

11:00 a.m.

The doorbell rings, I open and two policemen are facing me. My first thought 'They've come to arrest me because I've thrown my husband out ...'

They look anxious ... 'Beatrice?'

'Yes.'

'Your husband, Edward, has been found this morning by some passersby in a car as he tried to make a serious suicide attempt with the gas carbon monoxide into his car.'

Silence. My legs are about to melt or crack. I can't speak at all; I'm frozen on the hallway tiles. I can't feel myself, but I turned round lifeless, heavy, and rigid like a stone and lead them to the lounge. 'Are you sure? I phoned his school this morning and they told me he was teaching.'

A little confusion creeps up, but they double check the car number plate and the police report of the incident. They then asked me if I was expecting him to do that, so I tell them that we had some arguments and that I kicked him out because he'd been having an affair. Then I crumble in tears asking,

41

'Is he dead?' My words are not really audible, but they replied carefully uttering each word very slowly.

'He is in a hospital in Milton Keynes. Here's the number to find out … Is there anything else that we can do for you? Here are our numbers if you need us.' And they left.

I could barely speak to Juanita to tell her what had happened without bursting into tears. In the kitchen, an emergency British Gas Service guy was fixing the washing machine. This was surreal!

I rang Jane, she was strangely expecting that news and she offered to ring his school. I called Pearl at home, she agreed to speak to the head for me on Monday. I then rang Mum in Paris. Taking my courage in both hands, I dreadfully dialled the hospital number where he was at. The doctor I spoke to could not tell me if Edward was going to die or live. Panic follows as I do not know who to turn to. How will I get to see him? What will I tell the children? Oh my God, Edward, why?

Last night, I had made a 'divorce plan' on a kitchen napkin and now he was between life and death. I feel so hopeless, I would give anything to be near him and reverse the whole story. Is he going to die? Is he going to live?

Pearl came to visit me in the afternoon, which is what I needed and she sensed it. She had gone through separation and her words not only reassured me, but they helped to put things into perspective: 'Hold on, Dolly, with your divorce plan and putting the house on the market. Just wait, don't do anything hastily. Just wait.'

She had caught glance of my divorce plan written last night, like a shopping list, on the paper napkin. Pearl was about to become a very close friend and not just the old colleague from Renaissance High School whom I called at 01:00 a.m. in the morning while working or mopping the kitchen floor. Once she rang me at 11:00 p.m. from Tesco!

Pearl was still there when I rang the hospital to ask about any development with Edward's state. They were going to transfer him to Chichester Hospital where he would have a 'hyperbaric chamber oxygen treatment' to reverse the carbon monoxide poisoning. What do they mean? He was going to be airlifted because time was a factor. They still cannot say if he is going to live or die. The nurse was so sympathetic and humble on the phone. What was her name?

Life suddenly took a sharp turn without warning, without seatbelts. Is he going to die? Is he going to live?

Sue, Edward's mother, came down in the evening to London. On Monday morning, we left early to drive to Chichester, we got there at 12:00 p.m. Paul was flying from New York and would arrive on the Wednesday.

7

Between life and death

Tuesday
22.06.04

Chichester Hospital, Intensive Care Unit. He lays there, very white, the breathing machine tube coming out of his mouth, another tube coming out of his nose, many other tubes with different colours coming out of his chest, his arms, his hands … He looks dead. I cannot cope with the sight and run out, deeply disturbed, in floods of tears. All I can do is cry, I feel so lost, so hopeless. I do love him, I do love him, I do not want him to die! Is he going to die? No. He can breathe on his own but very weakly, the machine helps him. Really, what does that mean? Is he going to depend on this machine from now on?

Wednesday
23.06.04

In the hospital, he groans when the sedatives are reduced but does not wake up. He struggles, shows pain, but does not wake. He might be brain damaged. He does not wake. The bad news flow in like water from a running broken tap. The poisoning level was so high, he will probably have some lasting cerebral damage. He does not wake. I cry, I scream, I panic, I do not know what to do with myself. He does not wake. This desperate feeling is so deep into me; I can no longer control my emotions. From love and care to anger and desire to end it all with Edward and walk away. Sue comforts me. At times it helps; at other times, it does not. Paul landed that morning and arrived. He was so petrified but happy to be near his brother. I was glad to see him too.

The doctors gave us bleak news about his recovery in that afternoon. They could not say if he would ever return to normality because of his abnormal behaviour whenever they decrease the sedatives to try and wake him up. I got angry and hysterical that afternoon. I had been given his suicide letter the day before and shared it with Sue. I had found it quite plain in comparison with the letter he had written to his slut. That letter came to my mind then and I started to get really angry, really loud 'So, Edward, you want to say goodbye, fine, let's say goodbye! Paul, do you want to see the letter he wrote to his little fucking bitch? There, there it is (I tried to take it out of my bag, but he would not let me), let's say goodbye then!' I rushed to the door, but Paul and Sue stopped me. I was so angry and heated but hurt, agonising inside my veins, destroyed and hopeless.

**Thursday
01.07.04**

I spent the night in a room on my own. That was good, that night I let go. Late that night, I rang Sandrine, and with her encouragement, I just cried and cried as I had to empty myself from held-back tears in public. Why do we cry? Does it really make us feel better? That night, it did for me. Everybody kept telling me that what happened to Edward was not my fault, but I was the one who threw him out. I was the one who told him that he was 'less than nothing'! Nobody knows how I feel.

At the hospital, it's hope and despair. From Edward's reactions, Peter, the African consultant, tells us that 'It's not normal behaviour and there is some possible brain damage, but we do not know.' So I might end with a mentally disabled husband in an intensive care unit for a long time. He is taking too long to respond, and therefore, there is probably something very wrong. I am lost between sorrow and anger. I do love him, but I cannot stop thinking about the little slut who took my husband away from me and led him to feel so guilty that he tried to end his life.

What I had read on the Net about suicide helped me to understand a little more. Edward showed so many presuicide signs, but I did not know, therefore I could not see them. What am I going to do? What am I going to tell our children?

Later that day, I returned to London by train, to see my children, my sister Sandrine, and my au pair, Juanita. I left the rented car with Sue.

Friday
02.07.04

I returned to the hospital, there was no progress. Edward is still very agitated. His second scan shows as 'normal', we are all relieved. Back in London driving with Sue, bless her, we got lost at the start of our journey and made it home at 09:00 p.m. Yolaine, who had been looking after the children, was there waiting for me, as Sandrine went to collect our mum at the Eurostar. I will feel glad to have Mum here with me. Night after night, I feel depressed. I miss him so much. The pain is always there, very tight in my chest, and it won't go away. I now take so many pink pills to calm the palpitations and chest pains. They do not help, but I still take them.

Saturday
03.07.04

It is a beautiful sunny day in London today. I am with the children, Sandrine, my mum, and Juanita; we are trying to live normally. They are all really helping while I spend a lot of time on the phone trying to contact banks, insurance companies, and catching up with late bills to pay.

Later that morning, I lost my temper. I could not find the paper with all the phone numbers for the hospital. I was frantic, threw a chair out in the kitchen, kicked the table, knocked a flower vase on the table, it rolled and shattered on the floor. I had lost it! Sandrine came to see, grabbed me by the waist to calm me down, and in a minute, she found the paper. What was going through me then? This was so unlike me, what was going on? I could not recognise myself. I could no longer cope. The whole trauma was taking its toll on my strength. I was expected to carry on normally, smile, breathe, work, buy food for the kids when my husband was in a coma. Happiness is just a show, an illusion.

It's a down day for me, and friends who keep phoning me irritate me even more.

8

It's a miracle

Saturday
03.07.04
03:00 p.m.

Paul rings me in tears to say that he, Edward, called his name, blew kisses, hugged him. 'He woke up and he recognised me, Jane, and Sylvie on the photos! He's responded to the doctor's command!'

Paul sounded so overjoyed and emotional. That was a miracle; the day before, the doctors were talking about brain damage and he was still groaning and fighting, throwing his fists at everyone but still unconscious. I could not stay in London, I had to go and see him. So I left the kids with the girls once more and ran to take the 08:30 p.m. train to Chichester where Paul would be waiting for me in the station car park.

The train journey was long but filled with young and drunk people that time. One girl sat on my lap; she was so drunk and laughed about it for at least thirty minutes.

'I sat on that woman's lap.' It was funny and embarrassing at the same time. I got worried that they might make some racist jokes or comments, but fortunately, nothing happened. They were too busy trying to cheat on the ticket fares. I was quite relieved when the train arrived in Chichester and I met Paul—all smiles and bright eyes.

We went out for an Indian meal and tried to chat about a few things. In the new hotel, where Steve and Jane had already checked in, Paul then asked me to see the letter Edward had written to the slut. I gave him a copy, the original was hidden at home. He read it and understood my pain with a big sigh. What could he say anyway? He said it sounded like Edward was

47

finishing with her. Was I supposed to say, 'Thank you, Edward, how nice of you!'? It was not a suicidal letter. He wanted to tear it away, but since it was only a copy, it did not matter, and he took it with him to his room. I'm so unhappy but also hopeful for the first time. I have prayed so much during all those past days and pray again that God saves him. I made a pact with God: 'If you save him, I'll forgive him. Don't take him away from me!'

I struggled to fall asleep that night. I'm scared of being rejected. The conversation with Paul kept haunting me. We had discussed the future: separation or not, and our common goal is to see Edward heal. I prayed that Edward does not reject me tomorrow. I wonder if she came to see him, how would he react? Rejection? Why am I thinking about that? There is no way that little slut would have the nerves to come up to the hospital in Chichester! I am confused and upset, on the verge of a nervous breakdown, I think. I don't know. I don't know, I am really scared. I still love him and there is nothing I can do to stop that feeling. In spite of all the hurt, the pain, and the fear of losing him, I still love him. Is it bad love though? Hurting love? But, are we going to survive as a couple? Will I ever be able to forgive him? The future, if there is a future, scares me.

Sunday
04.07.04
05:34 a.m.

A fat fly woke me up as it was stuck between the curtain and the window. I could not find it, I could only hear it like an engine against the window. It buzzed in my ear for so long. I got out of bed to sort it out, but it hid right away from my sight. Why is this insect in my room tonight? Is there a message here I am meant to understand? I ought to let go of Edward, and even though he is desperately 'flapping' for his life, even though his 'ghost' is still brushing on and off against my troubled mind. The fly, Edward, the fly, Edward, I want them to go, to leave me alone. Love, desperation, trauma, love, betrayal, coma … It all went so wrong. Happiness is an illusion.

Sunday
04.07.04
06:37 a.m.

I dreamt of an old and luxurious apartment with a lot of communicating rooms that I wanted to purchase in Paris. I dreamt that I was dancing alone while Maman La was watching me, with a very amused look on her face, or maybe it was Edward. I cannot remember. The music was by Charles Trenet 'C'est si bon ...' Nothing was 'bon' at the moment, though. Maybe a macabre dance was waiting for me.

I still woke up very anxious, thinking that Edward would refuse to see me. After all, I was the last person he saw before attempting to kill himself. I was the one who kicked him out of the house, telling him he was less than nothing. I had told him how much I was sorry and how much I loved him while he was in coma; I hoped he'd heard me. What would I do if he rejected me? Probably run away, and that would be the end of us forever. I told Paul how I felt, so we made a plan. Paul would go in first and tell him that I was there, and then I would go in to feel him alive again ...

I barely ate at breakfast with Steve, Jane's husband, their baby Jack, and Paul. My chest was clutched tightly by invisible spiky chains I could not loosen. I needed a handful of beta-blockers right now! Outside the Chiswick Hotel, fancy that name, just like my London home area, but here in Chichester! The world is really not that big a place; the connections are everywhere surrounding us, coincidences or signs? My state of mind wanders back and forth to strange anxiety lands and returns to Chichester.

This morning, Jane and I spoke about manicure. Apparently, fake nails damage your real nails underneath. I did not know that! Jane suggested that I simply had my nails polished and pampered from time to time. It sounded like a very good idea, but when could I do that? We laughed a little. Nervous laughter, but I needed that, just for a few moments to be happy again.

Sunday
04.07.04
09:07 a.m.

The corridors to the intensive care unit seemed longer and whiter than usual. The ceiling lights were hurting my eyes with their brightness, or maybe my eyes were too sore with past tears and lack of restful sleep. We arrived at the coded entry doors and Paul went in while I waited in the relatives' room for his dreaded return. He did not take long, but he rushed back to me short of breath smiling and saying, 'He's asked to see you and he can't wait!' I stood up and almost ran to his room. My heartbeat was so fast, but with joy this time. I was joyful but trembling and apprehensive at once.

'I love my wife, where have you been? I love my wife' were his first words as he saw me. He shouted them out with tears running down the corner of his green eyes. He opened his arms and I just held him so tight. I could not let go of him; those strong arms were so warm and made me feel so secure. 'I've never stopped loving you, Edward. I've never stopped loving you!' I whispered in his ear. We held each other crying and sobbing for a long time. He was holding me like he'd never before, so tightly, so lovingly.

Around us, everyone was in tears—doctors, nurses, and family. We were so relieved to have found each other again. 'I'm so sorry,' he kept repeating over and over, like a prayer that was releasing him from his demons. He apologised in the middle of his tears, over and over. I did too. I was so happy. He was alive and would survive. 'You smell good, you always smell good; my wife is so sexy,' and we all laughed.

We spent all morning together. He was exhausted from trying to talk and would sleep or nod off. How could he have tried to kill himself? I did not understand and knew that many questions would have to be answered, but later. For now ... I was grateful to God and I would keep my word since he was alive, I would forgive him. Was that a good pact to have made?

I was so happy he was back with us. He seemed to have his mind back even though his movements and his speech were very slow. It did not matter to me. The truth is, I cannot imagine my life without Edward. When he asked me if I had missed him, he burst into tears again, saying,

'It must have been so hard, what happened will never happen again!' What did he mean exactly? He will never try to take his life again? He will never have another affair? He will never have an affair with her again? Then he said he wanted to renew our vows and he told Paul! So he had not forgotten about our promise back in April. Had he forgotten her?

I fed him at lunch. I gave him a flannel wash. That was very tender and intimate. Somehow, I felt like I was washing some pain away from his body. He was pleased to tell the nurses, 'My wife gave my wash so you don't have to do it,' with a wide grin on his face.

He displays at times some very childish behaviour, like wanting to buy a flat screen television as the one hung above his bed, 'Oh please, can we buy one?' That was very strange and neither Paul, Jane, nor I knew how to respond to that. We smiled, looked at each other puzzled, and said, 'Well that's expensive!'

'Oh? How much? How much?' he asked like a spoiled child.

'Five hundred pounds.'

'That's not too bad, we can afford that, can't we, Beatrice?'

'Um yeah,' I said hesitantly.

Something was happening to Edward's mind. He had gone back to being 5 years old; this worried me for a while, then that feeling went as the hopefulness of his recovery pushed away my anxieties for a moment or two.

I had to return to London, but I promised him that I would come back on the next day. He looked really sad and worried as I left. It was very difficult to part from each other, but I also needed to have some sort of normality by returning to Sylvie and Julien who had not seen me much recently between all my journeys to Chichester. I was so exhausted, drained.

Sunday
04.07.04
04:45 p.m.

I travelled on the train and I met an angel, her name was Julia. The 05:00 p.m. train from Chichester to London was cancelled. There I was in Chichester station not knowing where to go next. She appeared suddenly behind me and said, 'I think that there is a coach replacement service, and it's over there!'

'Oh, thank you. I'll just follow you then,' and I did. On the coach, she sat next to me and I told her how tired I was visiting my husband in the hospital back and forth. Then I slept a little on the coach till the station of Horsham. When we arrived at the station, I boarded onto the waiting train and she entered after me, with a big smile. I sat alone, miserable, and shattered; she came and stood in the alleyway, near me, and said gently, 'They serve rolls on the platform with cheese or ham, would you like one?'

'Oh yes, that would be great. If they have anything with ham,' I replied, surprised by her offer. She returned within five minutes offering me a sandwich roll and a cup of tea! I felt so grateful. She then produced some sugar packets out of her pockets, she was my angel and I told her. She did not accept the cash I was trying to give her to pay her back. But this was just what I needed, someone to take care of me. The journey was long and slow. A sweets trolley came along later, and I bought her a Mars bar as her 'dessert'. As we approached London Victoria, I kept thinking about how I could thank her for her kindness. On the platform, I went to her. 'Thank you very much for your help and kindness earlier, it meant a lot to me …' and as I could barely hold my tears, I looked away. She replied, 'Well if I could help a little then I'm glad,' she smiled and I left. I later saw her waiting on the same tube platform, but I was then far too upset to return and talk to her. Tears were flowing down my cheeks; my throat was tangled and I would not have been able to speak. The knots in my heart were too heavy and tight.

That night at home, I realised that praying, after all, had been the answer and I would keep my promise. For the first time in weeks, I fell asleep relaxed, looking forward to the next day.

Monday
05.07.04

I spent the day at home in London. In the morning, the children seemed contented, but Sylvie is worried about her daddy being in hospital. She asks me some questions but changes the subject if I touch on the 'Daddy is thinking about you even if he's been away.'

Julien is having some nightmares; he never used to. In the morning, he wakes up calling for his dad. What can I tell him? 'Daddy is ill, he will come home soon. Give a cuddle to Mummy,' and he does, my little angel boy. How much does he understand? Sylvie is so bright and mature for her age, how does this affect her? When will I know?

How could Edward want to leave such beautiful and adorable children? They are gorgeous, every day, everywhere, everyone says so from the mums in the park to the librarian or shopkeepers in town. They are clever, like their mother, I always say. Well, while I was expecting Sylvie, I remember reading one of those mum-to-be magazines, which said that the father determined the sex of the baby, but the mother passed on the intelligence. We are blessed with our children, they are totally perfect to us!

This morning, I received a very optimistic call from Paul: 'Edward is talking normally, even about his new job. I think that you have your husband back, Beatrice!' A real miracle. I visit Dr Greek at the surgery, a few hours later, near home. For the first time, I tell him that Edward's affair was with a 17-year-old student. He is speechless and we then discuss how the whole affair is a symptom of his mental illness. Dr Greek is very good at listening and decides to refer me to counselling as I have 'a lot of issues to deal with'. We discuss my feelings of love, care, anger, and hatred all directed at Edward for what he has done with that girl and for trying to take his life.

I have never needed counselling before in my whole life! Me? I'm a control freak! I am always in the power position; well not anymore. Since April 2004, I have stopped being in control of my private life, of my husband's feelings for me. How could he say that he loved me and lied to me so much? Is it possible that Edward's behaviour is all about mental illness? I truly struggle to understand.

Back in May, when I browsed on the Internet, I found that men who cheat on their wives primarily do it for five reasons: 'Loss of ego, misplaced anger, boredom, escape from emotional pain, need for nurture and intimacy'. It helped on the moment to understand, but it did not help to give me back the happiness I had lost.

Last night, Sylvie had decided to draw a picture for her dad: a field with colourful flowers blowing in the wind and in big letters above 'I miss you, Daddy, get well soon, love from Sylvie'. I had promised to give him the drawing when I returned to visit him. I folded it and put it in my handbag before starting the car.

I returned to Chichester late in the afternoon. I did not get lost! Felt quite proud of myself after travelling alone on the motorway like an independent woman who knows where she is going, almost. Something good came of this: now I can drive long distances on the motorway on my own! Silly but valuable. Next time, I'll go to Paris by car!

Paul welcomed me at the hospital and looked absolutely dreadful. He had not shaved and had spent all his time with Edward. He then described how Edward's speech faculties were deteriorating. He would talk normally, but any painful topic would literally stop the words from coming out clearly. He would then go into some sort of blurred speech very slowly and finally he would utter completely incomprehensible words. I understood what he meant when I saw Edward that evening. He was very uptight and angry about being moved into a geriatric ward! He was complaining about the nurse not doing what he wanted.

Edward's mental state then was very alarming. He seemed to think that everyone was against him. The whole world had a plot against him. It broke my heart to see him like that. He could barely express himself; I could not understand a word. He spoke slowly as though very drunk, but no words could be understood at all. It was so frustrating for him. I could see in his eyes that he knew what he was trying to say, but the words would not come out at all. I told him to write, but he could not even do that! He scribbled some letters and words which could not be read. I became so anxious but did not show it. Was he going to be completely insane? That was so scary. He is one of the brightest men I had ever met and there he was unable to speak, unable to write. What had happened overnight? From coma to that, I prayed that this was only a transition phase, it would pass, soon.

When he would take a break, a few words would come out clearly then the strange language would take over or he would even reach a stage when he would not be able to utter any sound at all. His lips would mime, but no words. This was so painful to watch. I had lost my husband again, or maybe he had never returned. Happiness is an illusion.

Remembering my Internet research, I recalled that the symptoms he had been showing in the early days of his treatment in the intensive care unit were an indication that he had been so close to dying in the car and had consumed enough carbon monoxide to leave him with permanent brain damage and even paralysed. Edward was not paralysed, but his speech functions were damaged. What I dreaded the most was the length of time this would take to be repaired, re-educated: a few months, a few years, and what if it was never going to improve?

Tuesday
06.07.04

I stayed with Edward that morning, Paul returned to London to travel back to New York on Wednesday. He was really devastated to leave, but there was nothing else he could do. He had to return to his family too. He had been at Edward's bed without a break and it was time to take care of himself. Now that his brother's life was out of danger, he felt more relieved. We said goodbye, both uncertain of what the future would bring to his brother, to my husband.

Back in his ward, one short conversation with Edward became a rain of revelations. I did not ask him for anything, he started to talk openly, I was surprised. He told me voluntarily and freely about the girl and what happened on the day they 'tried to make love in the open air'. He told me that they went for a walk in the woods, but he did not say where. Suddenly, she lifted her skirt for him and dropped her knickers for him! I nearly laughed and asked, 'What? She dropped them just like that? That's what kids do!'

'The whole thing was so embarrassing! I'm so sorry! I could not even get an erection!' he replied. I wondered if he was aware of what he was actually saying to me, his wife, the one he was meant to love and cherish and be truthful to. I just listened with a few questions in between. 'Did you sleep with her? Did you have intercourse?' He replied, 'No, no, I couldn't, it was so pathetic!'

Then he started to struggle with his speech and grabbed the notepad sitting on his bedside table. He tried to write while saying a few sentences and searching for my approval in his eyes. He wrote that he *felt like a toy to her, that Ariana became very manipulative towards'* him. I did not know what to make of all those revelations. I did not know what was true, what was fiction, what was distorted. He continued to write, struggling, *'I'm so sorry for everything, I'm sorry I did this to you. I wanted to die, that was my only way out. It became like I felt I did not have any time at school for my job. I felt I had no time in the day. The bottom line is NOT that I created the situation. The bottom line is, whenever I was busy, she would turn up to see me! It became so embarrassing!'*

I wanted to ask more questions like: 'Where did you meet? What did you do? Where did you go? Who saw you? Who knew about you?' My questions stayed in my mind, I knew that this moment would be a one-and-only confession time, so I chose not to interrupt him. He finally wrote: *'That summarises how she felt about me: I was her ideal fantasy present. She was emotionally immature.'* At 17, it must be thrilling and exciting to have a 41-year-old man infatuated with you. I did not entirely grasp all he wrote, the true meaning of his words being locked in his troubled mind. What am I to do with this confession? Forgive him? Understand the reasons why this whole affair started? Is he trying to give me some excuses to apologise for what happened? To be forgiven? I cannot think clearly. This would make her entirely responsible and would that be the truth? So she was that desperate for sex with him? Why did she need him so much? What was she hoping to prove to herself? To whom? I cannot see the point in all this, was she not scared of the whole situation? Obviously not, she had some fucking bloody nerve to carry on seeing him after meeting me. I concluded in my heart and mind that that girl was an evil spirit, goddess of destruction over time. But what was Edward? A monster? A manipulated man in mid-life crisis crap?

Surely, she must have known that it could not last, or could it? Thus, she could control herself with sexual excitement and had to give him the big signal 'let's drop our knickers off' and see what he does. Is that what she thought? What did he do then? I was left to imagine what followed since he did not say and had stopped writing, exhausted from his flow of revelations. I cannot believe that he lied to me here in hospital, but I still think that the whole truth was still to come out.

9

Return to London

Tuesday
06.07.04
02:00 p.m.

They have a bed in Charing Cross Hospital and Edward will be transferred in that afternoon, what brilliant news. No more long journeys for me, and the children will now be able to see their father. It has been nearly three weeks since they last saw him flying their kite in Wandsworth Park.

I phoned Paul to let him know. He was so delighted to hear that. It was only one hour since he had left the hospital, so relieved he could continue his journey back home knowing that Edward would be also closer to home and family.

The ambulance guys, Dave and Lisa, were very friendly, as they always are in my many experiences with them helping with Edward's hypos in the middle of the night. Why does he always have to go hypoglycaemic when I really want to sleep, or when it is really late and there is no sugar in the kitchen to make him come back quick enough? The man was so inconvenient with his poor diabetes management. I felt so many times like his nurse, rather than his wife.

Dave told me to follow them from the hospital's main entrance. I drove towards that main entrance, but they never came. I had time to argue with an old lady about my poor parking in the middle of the road: 'Look, madame, I'm only doing what the ambulance staff told me to do, I'm waiting for them!'

She mumbled something nasty and drove off. I felt stupid, though, as the ambulance never showed up. How many main entrances are there?

I resigned myself to drive back alone. I drove off and left the Chichester hospital to never return.

While on the motorway, I kept checking in my rear mirror for the ambulance, but never saw it. I stopped in a small service station to buy a can of Red Bull and some chocolate. What came over me? I never eat chocolate! I do not like chocolate! The cashier nearly charged me twice as I was holding a half-eaten bar of Snickers. 'Oh no, these I entered with! You can't charge me twice!' I was probably in a mood to argue with the world, first in the car park exit way and now in a service station. My periods were on their way out but 'Period woman', as Edward called me with my moods, usually takes longer to calm down and go away.

I arrived to Charing Cross Hospital at 07:30 p.m. 'Beatrice, where have you been? They waited for you!'

'I waited where they told me but they never arrived, maybe I got the directions wrong, as usual,' I replied quietly.

Edward was unpacking while mumbling and seemed flustered moving around his bed. He was complaining about his insulin being on the sliding machine. Not being able to control it himself was another hit to his already low self-esteem and he was becoming angry about it.

Apparently, the ambulance took ages because they did not have any A to Z in the car. That was a little foolish when you are entering London as a newcomer. A few moments later, a young psychiatrist came to see us and tested his reflexes. She asked him some thorough questions, I guess to see in which state of mind he was. Edward felt so happy to be taken care of at Charing Cross, near home. On his face, I could see the smile of 'Yes, I'm in London now.' She asked him if he still felt like killing himself, and he replied, 'Oh no, I'm so happy to be alive.' She continued with further physical tests. He was then asked to walk a few steps in the corridor and he could just about do that. His balance was weak and he had to take time to think before lifting each foot off the ground. The robot-like walk he showed worried me, but since the psychiatrist was positive about everything else, I did not think about it for too long. He would be assessed further in the morning. The nurses there were very friendly and caring. We did not speak to them for too long, but I felt reassured enough to leave Edward and go home to Julian and Sylvie. I was so drained; I needed a long, warm bath.

I had stopped taking care of me for a while, and I was starting to go very low on energy and moral. I returned home to the children, Sandrine, Juanita, and my dearest mother, Marine. It was late, Sylvie and Julien were about to go to bed; just in time for me to tell Sylvie that her daddy loved her picture and that he was now in London. 'So, can I see him?'

'Yes, darling, of course, maybe tomorrow if he is not too tired. But you know, as Daddy is very ill, he speaks a little funny and very slowly like that *Hullllo Syyylvie*. That must not worry you, it's only because he is ill. He will speak normally soon.' Well, I tried to explain to her how her daddy looked. She took that on and fell asleep with a cuddle and a smile. Little Julien was already tucked underneath his duvet snoring. I just kissed him on his forehead and left their bedroom. A deep sense of relief came over me that night and I went to bed. Never had the bath.

Wednesday
07.07.04

I have been off work for a few weeks now and colleagues have been sending me the most supportive e-mails. It is amazing how sometimes people can show compassion you never knew they had. Sent an e-mail to Mr John, my head, this morning to tell him not to inform staff about Edward's real situation, I cannot cope with sharing so much with people, it only upsets me. Although this makes me feel very lonely, it is better that way for now. Pearl still rings me; she is rock solid, adorable, and keeps an eye on me, even for far away.

After school today, Juanita and I picked up Sylvie with her brother and took them to see their father in the hospital. They have not seen him since 20th June in the park that morning. Edward was so happy to see them, he could not hold his tears back as he held them both very tightly against him. Julien was a little distant but still shouted 'Daddy' when Edward repeatedly asked him: 'Who's that? Who am I?' while pointing to himself. Juanita became really upset as we left. She feels for Edward and found it difficult to see him so frail and slow. I hope she stays next year with us. Who knows?

From: Beatrice Jones-Martin
To: Isabel Jones
09 July, 2004, 03:21 p.m.
Subject: Re Edward

Hi Isabel,

Happy to hear from you. Paul was really looking forward to return to New York, hope he had a good journey. I don't really know if I'm doing well ... Just hanging to a thin thread. If there is a meaning or purpose to all this, I am desperate to know what it is! I'm trying not to torture myself about the affair, but I cannot control my thoughts at times, recalling the lies and deceit ...

I can't help thinking that there is a timed bomb somewhere waiting to explode when she decides to talk out in the open about her relationship with Edward ... Or maybe she will not, but her best friend will?

Pray for us and remember to tell and show Paul how much you love him.

Love you lots, Beatrice x

Thursday
09.07.04

It's our ninth anniversary today, well, it was a week ago, but today we can celebrate. I sneaked into the hospital at 10:00 p.m. to give him something nice to eat and drink, alcohol free, of course. I stopped at the Thai market on the way to pick up some warm Thai salad, I couldn't resist it. The smell of the spicy prawns, the lemon, and ginger sauce in the ward was quite strong, but God knows how much we needed to eat something sexy. Thai food is the sexiest!

Edward could barely communicate with me. Words would not come out in spite of the great efforts he was making to try and articulate, I just could not understand him.

I feel so hopeless and so down. I only want him back with me. Will that ever happen again? It's now 01:30 a.m., I feel a little more hopeful. He cannot stay in hospital forever; he will have to come home!

From: Beatrice Jones-Martin
To: Isabel Jones
10 July, 2004, 00:49 a.m.
Subject: Re Edward

Hello again,

I'm still not in bed, I will seek advice from the Church as well as you suggest. I wish you were around because I really value our friendship, Isabel, thank God for e-mails! I did make a pact with God, I told Him that if He saves Edward (from dying) I will forgive him, so I guess I'll have to stick to my word now!

It's too early to think about separation. With the suicide dimension into it, it is like a very serious game where we could all lose! I really do not know. I think that I need Edward to admit to me that he was wrong, that he was also after her, instead of accusing her of being 'manipulative', I need him to face his wrongdoings and to stop hiding behind some sort of illness. He has a lot of issues in his troubled mind, but he is not completely insane or irresponsible of his actions!

I just want the truth, however hurtful it might be. The truth about his feelings (present, past, and future) will help me heal. But somehow, I do not think that I will ever get that! And this is what is killing me most, not knowing what he was really up to or what's in his head! You'd think that living together for ten years would mean that I know him so well ... I was so wrong. I never saw this coming.

I now have to deal with love, anger, sorrow, hope, and disillusion and continue to be a mother the best I can. That's not what I was planning on that certain wedding day when I said 'I do'.

Wish you never have to face such a mess. I will try to be more positive in my next e-mail.

Love X

From: Isabel Jones
To: Beatrice Jones-Martin
10 July, 2004, 00:52 a.m.
Subject: Re Edward

Truly, I do not think that I would have anything positive to say if I were in your shoes, so please do not apologise. Edward is a fool unable to make manly responsible choices. I am happy for you and for your family support around you; but I am not sure that hanging on to feelings for him is a good thing for you. You have been through so much that is incomprehensible and hurtful. Maybe you ought to try and protect yourself for your children and your sanity. He does not deserve you. I am here for you. With much love,

Isabel X

Saturday
10.07.04 01:22 a.m.

Feel so pitiful and so lonely. Feel like resigning from my job, feel like dying. Thinking back, Edward's speech problems seem to increase. It hurts me so much to see him suffer like that. I am so scared that he is not going to recover and will feel suicidal again very soon.

Saturday
10.07.04

God has a super computer and he read my e-mails last night! Today at hospital, Edward spoke nearly for three hours nonstop. We spoke about the future, our future, and how we believed in each other. He even opened up about the girl and answered some of my very personal questions: the night he phoned the Colliers Wood Hotel and went as he said to the piano bar, how he contacted her; again he spoke of how she dropped her knickers down and how they touched each other intimately and how he was embarrassed, etc. Strangely, I was not hurt or angry (this time), but just relieved and happy that he could talk to me about those things. As Isabel said, unless I know, I cannot close the book.

For the first time in two weeks, I feel happy tonight and it's raining hard. I wonder if he will continue to tell me the truth I so need to hear. God has got a computer, and he reads my e-mails!

10

Home sweet home

Sunday
11.07.04

I can barely wait for him to return home. Tonight at the hospital, he told me how he was 'indulging' himself, then he added, 'I was tempted to call her, she was sexually attracted to me.' Edward's description of his feelings for her is still, somehow, ambiguous. He was indulging himself in this relationship … Those words were battering my mind like a broken wooden shutter against a window in the wind. Am I fooling myself? Yet he also said with tears in his eyes, 'She was not you!' I do not know what to think and I am increasingly more and more confused. It might be better to stop this self-torture for a while and go back to live on, or pretend, so just for a moment, I can't wait for him to come home.

Monday
12.07.04

Already four weeks since Edward tried to kill himself. Pearl came to visit today, that was good. Pearl came to visit today, that was good. We had lunch together and Julien showed off his French and English switching skills for the first time. Pearl's straight talk and warmth make me laugh. For a few hours, she makes me forget the trauma and gives so much care. She kindly and generously gave some really precious moments of her time.

I returned to the hospital later that night. Edward's speech was slow again. Tiredness or because we discussed the girl? He really got upset when

I reminded him that I kicked him out of the house on the Sunday and this was how he ended up in the car. It was like a puzzle piece for him. I thought that he always knew that! This was the reason why I had been so afraid of his rejection when he came out of his coma.

He became very angry about her. I am starting to believe that he thought he had fallen for her. He called me his hero. Am I? He seems so determined to make it work between us, saying that he will never look at another student again or another woman. The whole affair is just so hard to swallow whatever he says and however upset he gets. I do not know where I am, but I know that I am unhappy.

Tuesday
13.07.04

My morning first thought: I'd better start to unpack his things. When I kicked him, I had thrown all his possessions in black bin liners for him to collect before the divorce. It didn't take that long to shove all his bits and pieces in the bags. 'No more bloody mess everywhere! No more shampoo on the bath! No more comb full of hair on top of the cupboard! No more shaving cream in the sink!' I was so mad that morning and so determined that there would be no compromise, no way back, no more 'forgive me darling for I have sinned'. What a load of crap!

And now, I have to unpack it all, otherwise, I might send him back to the suicidal car. I called Juanita to give me a hand and as she sees the amount of bags under the beds, she burst out laughing, 'Who's done all that?'

'Me! On the Monday morning, before the police came! It didn't take me long with a mad rage helping!'

And there she goes still laughing picking up funny objects from the bag she's holding with one hand. 'What's that?' she asks pointing out to an ear-cleaning bottle that Edward used once. We continue to giggle while hanging back shirts, trousers, and ties. I wondered if Edward would notice that his clothes were arranged differently, probably not. Together, we managed to sort it all out quite quickly. What would I do without Juanita?

She has been amazing in those past weeks. Really comforting me with her kind words or just a tap on my shoulder when I felt low. The children adore her, respect her, she is fun, imaginative, creative, and an excellent cook! I will miss the Chilean dinners that would surprise us on our late evenings, laid on the table. Juanita takes care of the kids like royalty and I could happily leave them with her for a weekend break, well I say that, but would I do that? Still, the idea is nice.

Tuesday
13.07.04 04:00 p.m.

At last he is at home. I am really relieved but also very anxious about our future, his healing mentally and physically. I have no doubt in my mind that Edward is really fragile and will be demanding. Will I have the strength to deal with him? I have always been able to cope with his mood swings and his temper fits, especially when he would say something really stupid and we would burst out laughing in the middle of an argument.

Edward is very possessive, domineering, and never allows me to be angry at him. He cannot bear it if I give him one of my 'I'm fine'. 'No, you're not fine!' He would shout out back at me, really loudly as though the loudest he was, the less grudge I would have against him, but he was always very wrong on that one! I hate his screaming and that Jekyll and Hyde personality shift he does. It makes me hate him at times, so badly I could hurt him, or me.

I remember once after a blazing row over nothing, as usual, he had been yelling and roaring about me leaving him, his habitual 'I can't get you to agree with me, so divorce me now'. Suddenly, the phone rang, and as he had picked it up, his voice became so mellow on the spot as he heard Isabel speaking from New York. The transformation was astonishing; I looked at him gobsmacked. From that day on, I think I stopped taking him too seriously with his anger fits. The actor in action had performed there and then in front of me: the perfect Jekyll and Hyde masterpiece! Bravo, Mr Jones-Martin, you are such a brilliant and a mean actor!

Since that show, I would completely ignore him and at times that would wind him up so much, but my lack of response would not feed his screaming, which was then reduced to moaning. All that was before the slut coming between us, before the suicide attempt, before his brain slowing his speech down, before destruction appeared, before hell dragged us down. We have gone so far down together that coming back up surely would be lengthy and probably a real obstacle course.

I am quite fit considering the stress I have been under. Well, stress is good to lose weight, and I look thinner everyday but I do not feel weak. Edward has lost weight too, but he looks ill and pale; ghostly. The tunes of 'The only way is up', 'Things can only get better', and the greatest of all, 'I will survive', often come to my mind when I am in one of those serious drifting moments. We have to sort this mess out. And there we are, I say the fatal and royal 'we'. It's a 'we' which really means 'I' in action. The 'we' is only an intention. Why do I always feel that I have to sort everything out? Complete control freak, but if I do not sort it out, who will? Not Edward! Not the kids!

In the evening, his speech slowed down again. I remember what the consultant had told us about the brain sorting out itself. The brain is more or less like a jigsaw puzzle, when some cells are damaged, it is like a broken piece from the jigsaw. The cells do not grow back to replace the damaged ones, unlike broken bones. The other undamaged cells will adapt their shape trying to do a best fit around the damaged cells, but that fit will take time to make sense to the whole brain system. When Edward's speech disappears, his cells are probably losing the connections and cannot make sense of the best fit yet. That's how I can cope with it, trying to think medically about it, however simple the explanation might be, it reassures me that overtime, he will be able to talk normally again. He spoke to Paul on the phone tonight and tried to thank him. Their conversation was very short, Edward could barely say a word, and he was far too emotional.

Bastille Day today and so is my friend Alex's birthday. I do not even have the time to buy her a present and feel really bad about that. She is 39 and I will text her later in the day. Alex is a fabulous woman, fun, generous, clever, and gorgeous. She has not found her soul mate yet, and I know that it gets her down at times, but I envy her freedom! She does not believe me but it's true. We met at Renaissance High School in 1996. Bill used to introduce his new staff to the students during assemblies, on the stage. Alex and I sat next to each other in that nerve-racking moment and she could not stop talking and laughing before the serious introduction started. It was so contagious. She could genuinely make anybody laugh, anybody happy. She and I became close very quickly, sharing our Caribbean origins, but she often calls me 'West Indian' with some of my old-fashioned principles.

'Come on to the party, Beatrice, it will be fun!'

'No, I'm not going, I haven't been invited!' I would reply.

'Yeah, West Indian! I'll tell so and so to invite you *personally* and then you will come!'

'Maybe?'

But I still would not go just because so and so felt sorry for leaving me out of the invites. I can be very silly like that and Alex certainly lets me know. I do not recall having an argument with her. How peculiar! Actually, I admire her so much, I don't think I would dare arguing with her, she would probably win.

When I was expecting Sylvie, I did not drive then, well I never needed to drive so I never bothered. Suddenly, the thought of being alone with the baby and not coping with an emergency led me to take driving lessons. Until then, I used to commute on the tube to get to Renaissance High. My bump gradually became huge, and one morning, Alex said to me, 'That's it, you're not taking the tube anymore! I'll drive you to school, you only live five minutes away from me anyway, and it's no big deal!' I argued with her, a tiny argument, that she should let me share petrol with her, at least. She never agreed. Every morning and every evening, she was my chauffeur. Sylvie used to kick me hard whenever I sat in Alex's car as if to say 'I know that voice from the womb'. We had a great time talking, moaning about work in the car, and most of all, laughing.

Today, she is 39, and all I can do right now is send her a text message for her birthday. I call her instead in the afternoon and apologise for lacking a present. She is not too fussy about her thirty-ninth birthday, the big one not to miss is next year and doesn't want to be reminded. I can understand that and then the forty-first could be a big tragedy, who knows. I ended the call with a happy feeling. That's Alex for you.

Sandrine and Mum have now returned to Paris, it is only Juanita who is left here to give me a hand with the children and Edward. Her contract finishes in a week, we are all dreading the goodbye moment. Must get her something really special as a leaving present. She came home today with some fantastic shots of the children with her. They really look like they had such fun with her, it is a warm feeling of peace that fills me up as I look through the pictures and select the ones I would like to keep, well all of them, but she disagrees. Edward is thrilled to see those pictures and starts to praise Juanita as though there was no tomorrow. He always has to overdo it; he is such a drama king! The smallest praise becomes a national award and the smallest problem becomes a planetary catastrophe, there is never a middle ground with Edward. Well at least, he has been talking normally to tell her: 'Juanita, you have no idea of how grateful we are. You are the best au pair we've ever had. I mean, some of them were awful, but you are really exceptional! You cook for us, you take great care of the kids and they love you ...' And it goes on and on.

Later that night, Edward and I decide to take Juanita out to a gorgeous Italian restaurant in town on her last day. Felt a bit cheap to do that, we loved her so much and yet we never took her out anywhere during the year. The truth is she was rarely at home during her free time—always out partying, and 'boyfriending'. Her English has really improved with such a busy social life.

11

Trial period

July 2004

Edward's health is gradually improving, but he still has those panic attacks where he cannot control his emotions. At night, he is scared of the dark, recalls the night in the car on June 20th. He managed to locate the police officer who found him in the car and thanked him on the phone. That was quite remarkable. How do you thank someone who rescued you from your suicide attempt and how can they believe that now, because you have saved them, you are happy to be alive? Only Edward could figure that out.

We had to cancel the Spanish holiday as Dr Greek advised him not to fly because of his breathlessness and the lack of oxygen from the carbon monoxide poisoning. We were all looking forward to that holiday. I had rented a magnificent James villa in a village near Alicante. It had a pool just for us, the beach was only fifteen minutes away, and the sun was going to shine for the whole of the two weeks in Spain. My lovely new summer pink linen skirt with matching shoes would have looked so light and inviting on an evening walk in the village … It would have been such a fabulous holiday, very costly too, but I wanted to do something different for us and for the children. With every holiday programme and holiday villas being advertised on the telly right since January, Sylvie kept asking, 'Mummy, can we go on holiday in a house with a pool in the garden?'

'No, darling, that's too expensive,' but one day, I gave in and phoned to make the great expensive reservation. Felt marvellous afterwards at the thought of Sylvie's smile when I would tell her. The dream villa is gone now, so I ought to prepare myself for the carefully chosen words I will use when I break the bad news to her.

'Daddy cannot take the plane because he is not well enough!' was the best I could do.

'Why can't we go without Daddy, like we did when we took the Eurostar?' she asked without a pinch of remorse.

'Because mummy cannot leave him out of her sight for one second, or he'll cheat on her again with a 17-year-old slut!' is what I wished I could say to my daughter, but instead I said, 'Because he will spend the holidays on his own and that's not very pleasant, he's just come out of hospital. We'll go to Spain my darling, but not this summer.'

'Can we go to a hotel somewhere nice, just for a few days?' she was really anxious that she would not have a holiday, which in Sylvie's terms means not going to a hotel somewhere nice. It does not matter if school is nearly over and the holidays begin, in Sylvie's mind, being on holiday means being in a hotel somewhere nice. So, I promised her that I would find a pretty place with a hotel this summer and that she would have a great time, especially as her French grandmother would join us early August. That did the trick. 'Mamie' as we call her in French is the funniest of all grandmothers.

Mamie Marine taught Sylvie to roller-skate, to dance cha-cha-cha, and to swim last Easter. Mamie looks younger than me and loves to hear 'Is that your sister?' when I try to introduce her to some English friends. She is returning in August to have a break with us and see how things are going between Edward and me. She has never really interfered in our marriage, but this summer, somehow, I can feel the wind of change. We shall see. I know that she has more to say than she seems.

From: Beatrice Jones-Martin
To: Paul Jones
21 July, 2004, 10:40 a.m.
Subject: Re Edwards

Hi Paul

Edward is OK. He still gets over-angry at very little things, such as not finding the correct teats for Julien's bottle ... He has such a temper which really puts me off and scares me at times.

On Tuesday morning, he saw the counsellor for the first time and it went well. I was with him till he started to talk about the girl and then I offered to leave, so that he'd feel freer to speak. Dying to know what was said though ...

Take care.

Beatrice X

12

A summer full of lust

Mamie Marine arrives from Paris, and two days later, Edward and I flee to a hotel in the heart of the New Forest. For the first time since the suicide attempt, we are alone and happy together. The brand new Peugeot has its chance to prove comfort and a little 'je ne sais quoi'; all I need is Thierry Henry sitting in the back telling me 'Va, va! Voum Béatrice!' Even though it's not a Renault. Edward was charming and so relaxed during the journey to Lyndhurst, only two and a half hours away from London.

This town is in the middle of a permanent traffic jam, but it is still picturesque. I guess that our freedom makes it look absolutely adorable. The old-fashioned shop fronts remind me of that small village near Cambridge where every shop only sold miniature tea sets in bone china. I had visited Barton back in 1992 with Nicholas, that posh boyfriend of mine. Well, Lyndhurst has probably very little in common with Barton, but it is still delightful and I am really enthused by the idea of discovering the forest.

Our room has a four-posted bed and seems to have been designed for sex all night long. Well, that is what has been on my mind as soon as I entered and I know that I am not the only one. After the fancy dinner at the sensational La Pergola, we returned to our hotel room. I sat leisurely on a very large and cosy leather armchair, pretending to read a few local magazines wearing my midnight blue déshabillé. My reading did not last very long. Somehow I was soon disturbed by the feel of some soft hands going gently up my legs, my inner thighs very, very slowly. Edward felt so good and we let our fantasies lead our moist bodies.

The hotel pool is small but still enjoyable. At 10:00 p.m., I had it all to myself as I left Edward in our room to gather a little strength for later. We both knew that this break was to regain our lost lust. We felt in love again and eager to please each other. The smooth music, the dimmed light, the teasing with the lingerie, he could not resist me, not even at breakfast, in bed. Edward was back to his sexy games and I was surely in a mood to play. We played all night, every night.

'Those horses just walk around freely!' I was totally under the wild charm of the nature of the New Forest. Driving through the thick woods, a group of horses was carelessly grazing by the side of the road, I completely fell in love with them, all of them. The atmosphere in the forest is heavy with the rich scent of humid moss in the early morning dew. The horses would then suddenly appear through the trees and surprise me with their majestic beauty. This is an amazing region and I wish the children were here to enjoy it with us. This is where we will take them for the 'holidays in a hotel somewhere nice.' Sylvie will not believe her eyes, Julien will be thrilled.

Edward was pleased to show off his forest-guiding skills as we embark on the walks from our cheap book of walks. When he suggested to make love in the bushes, I could not help saying 'Just as you did with her?' I had actually been thinking about their 'trying to make love in the open air' as soon as we had started to follow the first track. My comment annoyed him, but he did not get angry, fresh air has that calming effect on him. How can I forget? We were meant to be here to renew what we used to feel for each other, but how can I forget? The only hope I have is to pretend to be happy, to pretend that the slut was never around, to pretend that Edward never stopped loving me. In spite of all this, I'm thrown back into the torture at every street corner, at every supermarket, at every pub. There is always a girl who looks like her. Her face is so unattractive, so plain, and so common, she is everywhere. It is an everlasting nightmare I cannot awake from. How can I forget? I want to forget, but maybe I am not meant to forget. What was the purpose of constantly recalling such painful and disturbing memories?

Yet, the New Forest has taken us by surprise. We feel so much more relaxed now and start to wind down enjoying a nap on the hills, or a ploughman lunch in a remote pub in the midst of the purple heather fields. I love the English countryside with Edward, it feels so different from the Caribbean or France. Here, you can never be sure about the weather, even in the middle of August, and now in the New Forest, while you are snoozing on the hills, a herd of wild horses could suddenly gallop right next to your head. Edward laughs at my silly fears and agrees that we will never live in the countryside. The Parisian in me can just enjoy it for the time being, and that's long enough.

We spend a long time talking about our future. He wants to renew our vows. The idea has been in his head since the first time I found out about the affair. He had not forgotten about it, and even in Chichester, he had told a very surprised Paul, and that I had agreed to do that. I am not really sure and I will need to be convinced. Edward insists that it will be good for us, for the children, and even maybe for a third child. 'What? Are you out of your mind!' The romantic record just scratched in my head with a hissing sound!

I protested out loud in the fields: 'I am not going through childbirth ever again! The pain and the complications! No! Bearing Julien had been much too difficult, you don't remember do you? I do! I am not going through that again! We have a boy and a girl, that's it, job done, picture perfect! Got that?'

I hoped I made myself clear enough. Did I need to be so brutal? Probably not, it is simply in my tactless nature. The truth is that even if I would not mind having a third child, he was not to know that. Not yet anyway.

Back to our hotel room in the afternoon, I ring Mamie to know how my little angels are doing. I miss them. They are so fine, they do not even wish to talk to us. Before we left, Mamie and I had planned a programme for each day and it has been working very well. Julien has been jumping on the trampoline for almost three days in a row, at the leisure centre. He is so tired when he gets down that he can hardly walk straight. Sylvie has designed some artistic masks and has enjoyed playing indoor sports mania. Mamie loves taking care of the children without us around. They are not missing us, so they must be having a great time.

It is our last night in the New Forest and we have to make the best of it. Romantic dinner in the Italian restaurant nearby. I lose my ten fingers in a dish of grilled gambas, absolutely exquisite paradise seafood. The creole in me was in Heaven! Edward enjoys his game steak with Mediterranean vegetables. We talk about food, our children, our life together, our true feelings for each other. I know that we can make it work again, we must be able to. The world has only got to look at us now to see that we are soul mates, made for each other. He cannot take his eyes off me and I'm dying to smell him when I bury my face in his neck. That's because it's him, that's because it's me, as Montaigne would say.

When we come out of the Italian restaurant, it is raining hard on our shoulders. Never mind, he covers me under his coat, and we rush to the car. I feel so secure in his warmth of his arms, but will this feeling last? There is a couple outside under the porch, she is crying, he is trying to make her go back inside. She does not trust him anymore, he looks ashamed but not sorry. Maybe they also have a same sad story between them.

It is our last night and we make the best of all nights, in the shower, in bed, on the floor, on the sofa, well, he takes me everywhere. He sensationally takes my body to make it his property to pleasure and love in every inch. Edward knows how to take my time, how to make me wait, how to make me rush and slow down again. He knows how to play before making me explode in sweat and deep, deep pleasure. Making love to Edward is like a fountain exploding with fresh waters running down my warm body. I did not know that I had so much lust-making energy inside of me, it must be the rain. It reminds me of our wedding night.

A gorgeous and scorching heat escorted us on the wedding day, but thunder and lightning chased the heat away during the night. We made love as lightning was tearing the sky that night. Nine years later, tonight, we can feel the same overwhelming joy to give ourselves to one another, in the rain, under the Lyndhurst dark starry sky.

We spent our last morning shopping for unnecessary jolly pretty things such as antique books and sugar pots. Edward and I split for a while in different directions, I head for 'The Old Apothecary' with its antic jewellery and old-fashioned perfumed bottles and Edward heads to… Well, I do not know where to. Maybe another antique bookshop or a phone box? No, not after last night, he could not possibly do such a thing, that would be monstrous. Some dark thoughts came to my mind for an instant, but I did not want them to spoil my romantic break so I let them go away.

When we meet again, we hunt for another hotel which would be child friendly and free for next week as we are definitely returning with the children and Mamie. That will be the perfect holiday place for Sylvie, with a hotel to stay in. We find a friendly hotelier, with a reasonable price and child insured. On that great news, we leave Lyndhurst with the promise to return for more fun with the family. I long to see Sylvie's face when she will find herself so close to wild horses. And, Julien, he will not believe his eyes. Mamie will surely enjoy the change of scenery from London. After all, she has not visited England in great depth. She knows and loves Whitstable, especially the seafood restaurant next to the only cinema in town, and she visited us in Belmont when we moved in together. She will love the New Forest too.

Back in London

Edward was draining energy out of me, he is so demanding, almost like a child. I have many times told Yolaine that I had 'three' kids. He has been very tense again since our return from the New Forest and I wonder what he has got up his sleeves to make me scream in horror very soon. Maybe, he is nervous about meeting my cousins who are coming from Martinique for just two nights. I was desperate to do something for me too, so when Caroline phoned me to say that she was on holiday in Paris with her family, I could not resist inviting her at home. Last time we saw each other was at Easter 2001 when we spent some time in Martinique with Sylvie for her first trip to meet her Martinique family.

We spent a very touristy weekend sightseeing in London, and they loved it. Over the weekend, Edward excelled himself in his guided tour on Saturday but was exhausted on Sunday and stayed at home. I was left to pretend that I knew everything about London from St Paul Cathedral's building dates to the National Theatre. Had to call Edward on the tour to check a few historical dates and answer some tricky tourist questions. I suppose that when my family visits me all the way from Martinique, they are probably quite impressed with my ability to mix into the English way of life. A part of them must be astonished that I cope with the cultural shock they experience when they first arrive. The reality here for me is different. I do more than coping. I live here because here I am free: free from anyone who might want to judge me, free from some bad memories, free from the restrictions of living on a small island. I am not sure that they would understand if I shared those feelings with them. I live here because I chose not to live over there. I like being a foreigner here and yet it is also home here.

That's it, the car is finally loaded, Mamie is seating in the back with the children, Edward and I will share the driving. They are all so excited and joyful. 'We are going on a summer holiday' comes to my mind and I start singing, not for too long as I am told to be silent very quickly. The New Forest welcomes us with a short-lived sunshine and soon Wellington boots and rain coats become an extra item on the local shopping list. We walk in the mud, in the sand, in dirty waters, in the woods, and we get lost too, but it's a fabulous holiday and we couldn't care less. Sylvie is delighted with her hotel room and Julien still plays with Thomas the tank engine as soon as he wakes up.

Edward and I are still having great sexy times together as Mamie offered to swap her double bedroom for the large family room with the kids. This time, I have refined the show using the lighting to enhance my curves after carefully watching one of those saucy programmes about sex tips for girls. He is blown away with exploding desire and can hardly contain himself. 'Where did you learn to do that? You are so incredibly sexy and ...' there is no time to talk, my lips cover his mouth with the most sensual kiss ... We make love slowly, deeply, and I fell asleep in his arms.

13

The small alarm bell

End of August '04

I launched the idea of a day in Brighton before returning to the New Forest and Alex got hooked with Magdalena, another close friend from Renaissance High School. Magdalena would be with her lovely 4-year-old daughter Isa. Magdalena knew about the June trauma and the affair, but I did not tell her the mistress was 17 and one of his students. I am not sure that she knew already, but I was not prepared to tell her, not yet anyway.

We all ran to catch the Brighton train in Victoria station, split the bunch of kids and adults on different packed coaches. The day was promising to be very exciting. I had spent the night before shopping for fancy snacks and making healthy sandwiches. Edward did not really help and that was the best thing he could have done as I was in one of my 'don't make any suggestions, I know what I'm doing' moods.

Brighton was crowded as expected on a sunny August day, and full of Londoners. The pebbles disappeared under the masses of people of all shapes and sizes. I could barely hear the waves I dreamt of relaxing nearby while planning this day out. The smell of greasy chips and fried chicken teased our nostrils till we gave in to the fatty food. Somehow, the chips tasted better when bought by the sea, it must be the sea salt they sprinkled on them, or I wished they did.

Edward was very distant, very antisocial. He barely spoke to me, or my friends. Mum observed him in silence and I could see the look of disapproval staining her juvenile face despite being in her early fifties. She dared not say a word, but she felt embarrassed for me and I was mortified inside. He read his paper, buried himself in a fake sleep, never helped with fixing the bright yellow parasols. What was he thinking of? Who was he thinking about? I tried to ignore him, to put on my brave Beatrice face, but all my thoughts viciously made circles around one idea: I am fooling myself. The day went by with the kids laughing, crying, and running on the shore and me pretending to be relaxed. Who was I fooling? Alex, Magdalena, or Mum? Probably none of them. They all looked at me with interrogations in their eyes I could not respond to. I was ashamed, too ashamed of Edward's behaviour, too ashamed of myself. The promise I had made to God, I no longer wanted to keep but I felt trapped. This man was going to destroy me and I seemed unable to shout and scream 'stop', I was too ashamed.

'I need to go for a walk, I am going to see the art gallery by the peer, will be back shortly.' On those words, Edward awkwardly stood up and left. He struggled to climb up the sandy hill and his dark blue shirt disappeared in the crowd. Was he really going to the art gallery? I wanted to follow him, but I would have needed to justify myself and there is no way Beatrice would show any sign of distress in public, especially not in front of her mother. So, with burning knots in my heart, in my chest, on my soul, I let him go away.

Three hours later, he still had not returned. Now I had to share the worry but not my true hot red burning anxiety. Did he arrange to meet the slut here? Was he fucking her somewhere in a dark alley, against a wall, since they failed to do it in the field? What field anyway? After a brief discussion with the girls, I left them to go and hunt for Edward, alone. Trying to find that man on Brighton beach in the middle of the afternoon, on a sunny day, turned out to be very challenging. Of course, I could not spot him anywhere, and if the slut was around with him, they would not be sitting casually at a café, would they? Instead, I found some drug addicts, very high and very happy to see me wearing my tropical turquoise sarong. I also found some unusual creatures,s male or female, I was not able to tell but they smiled at me without seeing me. You need all sorts to make this world, and they were all gathered today in Brighton on that sunny afternoon.

I started to panic, Edward was not on the walkway, not on the beach, and it was getting late to return to London. I went to the coast guard's office. A charming officer took his description and I certainly made it clear that I was worried, not because I imagined that he was meeting his little slut around here, but because of his illness, maybe he had fainted somewhere in a dark corner. He alerted his colleagues and the search began from the tower, and on the ground. The guard tried to appease me, saying that he'd probably got lost, that it's very common, but I was not listening. We looked for my husband in the beach bars, in the beach cafés, and then I suddenly saw him walking towards the art gallery. The guard smiled and left me to run to him.

Anger and shame were almost making me choke. Where had he been for three hours? He protested his innocence that had been reading in a bookshop on the hill but had lost our spot and could not find the yellow parasol anymore. That bloody parasol kept blowing away, so I had closed it! He said he rang my mobile, but I did not answer. Have you tried to hear a mobile phone on a beach full of sea lions, idiot? I was so mad at him and did not know what to believe, once more: was I fooling myself? We argued as we walked back to the girls whose stare I could feel prickling on my skin even though they were miles away. I accused him of constantly embarrassing me in front of my family and friends, if he was no longer interested in us, he only had to say so and walk away. He replied that he was sorry, but he was truly lost after the bookshop and did not mean to cause so much pain. I felt sorry for him, for myself, we would never be the same again. The loving trust was vanished. The New Forest romance died away in three hours. Happiness is a fucking illusion. I must accept that to survive and live again.

14

Patching up time

Mamie left us to travel back to Paris on August 24th. The night before, she had tried to have an open discussion with Edward, but it finished in a total failure and one of his temper tantrum mini fits: he stormed out of the room. I pretended not to notice anything whilst putting the children to bed upstairs. When I came down to the kitchen, Mamie was so uptight, I thought she was about to physically explode. Her jaws have always been the first noticeable sign of her internal boiling anger. Her face hardened with her jaws completely immobile while her chin and throat became one. She was in total disbelief about Edward and did not know how to tell me how she felt. Yet, she was thinking so loudly that I could hear her thoughts: Edward was going to hurt me more. She was feeling so hopeless unable to protect me.

She had to let go and let me find out for myself, but that was really unconceivable for her. Mum has always had to control even though from a distance, her opinion and influence over me were undeniable. She did not have to say much, but when she disapproved of something, I could sense it deep down in my bones. A strong conflict was making her uncontrollably dissatisfied. How to reconcile her need to see me happy in my marriage and the truth that my marriage was ending in front of her powerless eyes? She painfully had to let go.

This last week in August was quiet but strangely ominous. We were preparing for the new term and trying not to think about the trauma of the summer just gone. Maybe there was some hope after all. Edward was returning to his old self, a loving father and a fun husband. We went for walks and got the house ready to welcome our new au pair, Rose. I had interviewed her over the phone and we were quite anxious about meeting her.

I collected Rose from Eurostar with Sylvie. She was standing near the arrival hall with her big black suitcase as I approached her from the back, I asked gently: 'Excusez-moi, êtes-vous Rose?'[1]

'Oui, c'est moi,'[2] she replied with a very shy voice. I was pleased to meet her at last, after some confusion over her train time. Rose was fresh and looked so French, a real contrast from our previous Chilean Juanita, our West Indian Beatrice the year before and our Tunisian Fatima before that. Our next au pair might be African or Japanese. It is good for the little angels to be open minded, except that we did not do diversity on purpose, it came naturally to us.

I spent the first week training Rose on the children's habits and routines. She was interested in the family but seemed to lack confidence with the children. She will have to just get on with it next week when we are back at work. I constantly thought of Juanita and how wonderful and proactive she was. I guessed that Rose was very different and would take longer to settle. She was extremely gentle with the children and they seemed to take on to her rapidly, things could only get better.

From: Isabel Jones
To: Beatrice Jones-Martin
29 August, 2004, 00:52 a.m.
Subject: Memories

How are you all doing? When I think about, I often feel the warmth and love of the special picnic lunch we had in your garden with your French friends, or the beautiful Thanks Giving dinner you had prepared just for us. Your house was amazing, with the fabulous lights and adorable scents everywhere. It was great being in London near all of you. New York is a beautiful city but I miss the special family atmosphere that we had all together in London.

---

[1] 'Excuse-me, are you Rose?'
[2] "Yes, that's me"

From: Beatrice Jones-Martin
To: Isabel Jones
30 August, 2004, 09:02 a.m.
Subject: Funny

I'm really happy that things are going so well for the girls. They are so bright and gorgeous, you are really blessed. It is true for me to say that Chloe and Hannah have inspired me to have children as they have always been so impressive from day 1 when I met them. And now, are great role models for Sylvie and Julien. Sylvie, in particular, worships her 'cousins from New York!'

Your last e-mail was very kind, as usual, and I must say that I do feel closer to you too. I often tell Edward that I miss you and our chats about the Jones boys. We definitely had fun together, and you know what? The bus 137, which stopped right outside your front door, has also got a stop near our house here ... The girls could have just hopped along to meet each other had you been able to stay in London ... I certainly remember those days you mentioned with my friends in the garden in Putney and the dinner we had together at Christmas.

The way you remember the house is quite something, candles always warm me up in winter, it must be the soft light! I love our home so much and if we had to sell it, it would really break my heart ... But there you are. Hope that we'll do more dinners like that in the near future.

Our new au pair arrived this weekend. She is friendly enough but not yet fully familiar with us. Hope it will work out and that she will be as easy going as our previous one. Well that's the news from me.

Take care,
LOTS OF LOVE
Bx.

From: Isabel Jones
To: Beatrice Jones-Martin 31 August, 2004, 01:05 a.m.
Subject: News

Thank you so much for your kind words about the girls, they love their London cousins too you know, and often talk about them. I hope that all will turn out well with your new nanny. Some help round your home and kids can only be a good thing. It is time for you to have some peace. Are you still planning to sell and go back to Paris or Martinique with the children? I will be very sad to see you leave, but totally understand if you do. Sometimes the most drastic decisions turn out to be the best ones.

Love,
Isabel

From: Isabel Jones
To: Beatrice Jones-Martin 2 September, 2004, 03:33 p.m.
Subject: School

Wishing you all the best for your return to school. It will do you so much good to be amongst young people again and their positive energy. I know you love teaching. Is Edward returning to work as well? I know he was talking about different options with Paul. Stay in touch.

Love
Isabel x

15

A new life about to start

September '04

I start work with the new teachers' induction day. The little black top and the little black skirt with the light pink linen jacket on top will look just right, not too uptight, not too fun. The new teachers recognised the efforts we made to make the day interesting for them without loading them with too much information. I have to make a good impression as the human resources senior leader, and the first person from the main school who welcomes them officially. The morning concluded with a French lunch on the house, well appreciated by all. Communication and a big smile always make the day go smoothly.

I was glad to return to work. Last July, I missed the end of the term for three weeks with Edward's suicide attempt. This September was going to be my big come back; Beatrice had survived the summer trauma and was ready to challenge the world again. Work meant a lot to me. I loved being at the forefront, talking to teachers and staff. The adrenaline shot just made me surpass myself and I would become someone else. I guess work felt like a stage and I was acting a part of it. Not showing my true emotions, my real fears of getting it wrong but pretending with a big smile that everything is always fine. I had to be in control and no one was to know how tough my life had just been, only Pearl knew the true me. I had to make a big come back, and I did, I was proud to show her. All the training days went really well and our highly demanding new head teacher, Mr Maurice Leon, was very pleased with the start of this new term.

Mr Leon is a very interesting character in his late forties, very short and slim, but his personality was very impulsive and passionate about his work.

He had started the previous term as a hand-over with Mr John. I had missed most of his arrival to the school and only heard about his reputation. He was full of hope for the school future. At times, it was quite mind-blowing to follow him, he could be so bloody fast in everything he did or even in the way that he spoke. Syllables and words go through his mouth faster than breath. Well, working with Mr Leon would be extremely different from working with ultra laid-back Mr John. If I could make big mistakes with Mr John, I did not feel so confident with Mr Leon, he was more demanding and asked for fast and accurate performance. Had no idea whether or not I would match up his expectations, but then who could?

Edward passed the occupational therapy Gestapo style interview and started at his new school. He was over the moon with his promotion as a head of faculty. He now felt that we were now two equal school senior managers. Why did it matter so much to him? If my salary was higher, so was my share of the mortgage and the bills. I do not think that I will ever understand this manly need to earn more than their female partners and the devastating effect on their ego when we, female and ambitious creatures, earn more. I am not a psychologist, but time and lifestyles evolve. Have they forgotten to evolve with them?

Anyhow, Edward seemed much happier at the Clergy High School in Surrey. Every day, he was praising the warm welcome he had received from his new head, his colleagues, and new students. The transformation was amazing. I still feared a catastrophe, but he was coping well with his new role and we had fewer arguments about work. Was that too good to last? A new style of leadership team seemed to suit him much better, his decisions were approved by his new boss, James Brandon, and more importantly, by his new head teacher, Richard Cleveland.

Richard had a very gentle way with people and always seemed ready to listen to you; well, that is how he sounded to me when I called him in July to tell him about Edward's suicide attempt of June. He had been very sympathetic then, caring, maybe because of his religious school, or simply because he has a high level of emotional intelligence and understanding of human behaviour. His voice was very calming and at the time, I thought I could tell him anything about Edward, but I retained myself. Instead, I spoke of the implications for the new post he had not yet taken.

Richard had been so supportive and kind, but yet concerned about his own legal position as well as Edward's recovery. I wanted to share the whole truth with him, but I did not dare tell him about the slut, I was too ashamed. At the end of our first phone call, I felt so dirty for lying, or for hiding the truth. How could I have told him that Edward had tried to kill himself after I kicked him out of our home, after I found out that he was still seeing the slut, and had sex with her, even after I had forgiven him at Easter? I hardly knew him, and there was nothing else I could have done or revealed. Richard had been charming, and throughout the summer, he had stayed in touch with us by phone. At last I knew that Edward's new boss would care for him.

16

The long shopping trips

Why does Edward always take so long to go to the shop round the corner or does he always have to have some time out from us when we go out with friends and family? The mystery question that really irritated me so much. I am sure that it does not require one hour to purchase some tablets from the local Tesco and the chemist. He has always made me wait, as far as I could remember.

On our honeymoon on the south coast in France, August 1995, the wax models of slaves enchained in a boat, at the History of Slavery House, distressed me so brutally that I had to run outside to catch my breath and thoughts again. There had not been any warnings for the sensitive souls, and to suddenly find myself from the antique paintings gallery to the slave ship was totally unexpected and troubled me deeply. Edward never offered to come with me outside to comfort me, so I foolishly left Edward inside thinking that he would want to join me back outside shortly. Well, how wrong had I been! I waited for three hours! I went window shopping; it was lunchtime in France, and outside the big cities, this is the dullest time of the day. Only a few cafés and sandwich bars were open. Edward forgot that I was with him, he forgot that we had just got married, he forgot that we were meant to be inseparable from now on! How innocent and naive was I! Three hours alone on the south coast in France, while Mister got engrossed in an eighteenth century play.

Now in London, in 2004, very little had changed and Edward still made me wait forever whenever we had to part from each other. In my mind, we were parting for a few seconds, but it usually turned out to be for at least forty minutes to one hour. That is just so bizarre, and it's more and more frequent. This would happen at the supermarket, between the aisles, in petrol stations, public loos, or in restaurants. Where did he disappear to? Why?

89

17

Now I know why

For the last week or so, Edward has been behaving very strangely. He seems constantly on edge and said that he's feeling the same way as he did in June 21st. He is feeling suicidal again, but why? We have been sharing the new car, the spacious Renault, and he drops me to work some days. On our journeys to work, he talks about how 'bad' he is. Truly, I have no idea of what he means, so how can I help him?

When he returns to pick me up, he is all over in the car. He hardly says hello to throw his lips onto mine, his tongue wiping my face, his wandering hands down my shirt, or below my skirt! His piercing eyes firing passion darts at me, but I honestly do not recognise this elevation into sudden sexiness in the school car park. What's going on in his mind? Edward has always had that unpredictable lover mood, but at 05:00 p.m., in the car, that's quite something unusual. We have been swinging between miserable mornings and passionate afternoons. Well, I do not mind, except that I would like to get time to relax from work instead of being jumped on in the car! And the contrast goes on.

At the weekend, his tolerance of the kids gets shorter and shorter, and the snapping gets faster and faster. In my heart and soul, I can no longer know this man. It is now completely impossible to predict how he will react to anything. I thought that we were getting better, well everybody did, but I was not so sure anymore. Something was coming.

18

Sad Tuesday

Tuesday
14.09.04

Edward's mobile phone was on the kitchen table. It must have been 08:30 p.m., the children were upstairs. While he was clearing the sink, I picked up his phone and started to look at his recent calls. That number ending 333 made my heart sink, it was hers, I recognised it straight away and nearly dropped the phone on the floor. He looked at me puzzled. 'You've phoned her! Today! She's phoned you back too! Edward, why? Why?' I was more devastated than angry.

'I don't know why. I- I am so sorry. I won't do it again, promise, please don't leave me! Please. I met her this afternoon in Chiswick. I wanted to tell her that it was over.'

'In Chiswick, when, at what time? Weren't you at school?' I asked more and more intrigued, sadder and sadder too. I kept shaking my head in disbelief. Surely, this was a nightmare and I was going to wake up very, very soon. But no, it was real and I could hear him say, 'No, I don't teach in the afternoon so I called her to meet her. I texted her and she agreed to see me.'

'Didn't she think it was a trick from me? How did you manage to get her there? So, she truanted school as well?' I could now feel the fury reaching my throat.

'Yeah, she first thought it was you but I insisted and she came.' His voice was so low, like a child caught red handed with nothing to back up any claims of innocence.

'And? And? What happened? Did you kiss? Did you fuck her, at last? Were you pleased to see her? Was she pleased to see you? What happened? Why are you doing this, after all we've been through? Why? You can't live without her? You're missing her?' Anger was now coming up my veins and pouring out of my skin like an enraged blood river bursting out of my mouth.

'Yes, I miss her music.'

'Oh fuck you! Her music? Damn me if I can't play an instrument, I'm not good enough, not artistic enough! Fuck you and go to hell, you and your little slut!' And I turned my back to him to walk away from him, but he screamed at me in agony: 'Oh please, Beatrice, it's not like that! It's not what you think!' He went down on his knees and started to hit his head with his fists. He was sobbing, crying, scratching himself, a real display of hopelessness, but I was not impressed at all, not this time. Deep red anger had consumed me and left me dead inside.

I was less fiery than before; I was feeling truly defeated and powerless this time. They had met in Nando's, how romantic and cheap! But that's just up the road from us! Why didn't he invite her at home while I was at work? That would have been easier, cheaper, and quieter! Our bed is very comfortable, they would have had a hell of a good time fucking each other upstairs, in MY bed! She is like a bloody leech getting closer to me each time. I glanced at the floor and saw that he still had her photo again in his bag. That bloody article about her musical prize, I took the newspaper and tore it in front of him. Her face gives me the creeps. Seeing her again made me feel physically sick. Tearing her into bits of paper made me feel good, but what did it change to the way he felt for her? Probably nothing. I cannot even qualify it or understand it.

Midnight, I had to do something, something real with an impact, so I made him call her. No reply so he had to leave a message: 'Hi Ariana, it's me. Look, we mustn't see each other again; Beatrice has found out that we've met today. I don't know how, but she has and we must not meet again next week or ever.' He did not say that HE did not want to see her anymore, I had been dreaming in silence while listening to his pathetic voice talking to her voicemail. Then I took the phone off him to leave my message to her as a last sentence: 'Ariana, this has to stop, it has to stop, he's tried to kill himself, he is not well, and this has to stop. Well, if it doesn't stop, I don't care anymore.' What else could I have done?

I spent the rest of the night trying to calm him down, preventing him from opening his skull on the walls. He called the Samaritans, but they were not helpful, just pushing back time before another drama. Had Edward lost his mind? What was I to do, to think? Tomorrow would be better, surely, it has to get better!

19

Lost illusions

Wednesday
15 09 04
04:00 a.m.

After two hours in bed, I got up. Not sure, I had slept anyway, and like a robot, like the first time, back on June 20th, a strange force was pulling me to search his bag. He had slept on the sofa downstairs. Marital bed had ended abruptly last night and I did not feel it would ever return.

I found what I was looking for: a letter. It read:

Ariana,

I've settled well to The Clergy High School. Very well in fact. Met all my students. Already have plans for staging plays in a number of theatres. The Brown Roof Theatre is a strong possibility.

We're going to see a production of the A cat on a hot tin roof in October soon and I was hoping to catch you in London that night. Alternatively, I am free every Monday from 02:15 p.m. Can we meet next Monday somewhere? Probably best if I meet you somewhere in London, let's say at 03:00 p.m. ... or in Victoria if you can get there ... Let's say London at 03:00 p.m. next Monday. I'd love to spend some precious time with you then return to my boring home for 06:00 p.m. Or I could meet you near home! You once told me that you could get there direct ... Let me know. If it's Chiswick I could get there quicker. Can't wait to see you. I have so much to tell you. Missing your music so much!

E.

What more could I say or do, she wins, again and I lose again. I e-mailed Paul, but what's the point? What will that do? What is it going to change? The truth is that nothing has changed since 20st June 2004, Edward is still obsessed with her, she is on his mind and I am completely powerless to reverse that situation. Even making love twenty-four hours a day would not resolve anything, except maybe my fitness level. I have to resign myself to realise that it's over between us and we are just living in our lost illusions.

From: Beatrice Jones-Martin
To: Paul Jones
15 September, 2004, 06:09 a.m.
Subject: He is back with her

Well Paul, all was well until I found the girl's number as a recent call in Edward's mobile last night. Then he also told me that he was planning to meet her again yesterday. I also found another copy of an article with her photo on front page in his bag. He was 'going to give it to the new music teacher' ... He is really taking me for a fool! Maybe I am. Very big trauma followed, he felt so small when I caught him. He was behaving like an insane person and kept saying he wanted to die without taking his breath between sentences. I made him call the Samaritans at 11:00 p.m. last night. When he calmed down at midnight, I forced him to call her and he left a message on her mobile saying that I had found out about their meeting and that they should never see each other again. Then I also spoke after him and told her: 'Ariana, this has to stop, it has to stop, he's tried to kill himself, he is not well, and this has to stop. Well, if it doesn't stop, I don't care anymore.' This morning, 06:00 a.m., I've just found a love letter he wrote to her, in his bag. He is 'missing her music so much, going to be in London and hopes to meet her etc. . .' He has been lying to me again, actually, he never stopped lying. After the entire traumatic experience he's put us all through! He cannot be without her! That's quite clear. He did not want me to tell you, but I don't care anymore, Paul. He has ruined my life enough! Separating will make me unhappy, staying with him will make me unhappy too. What should I do? I feel so used …

Beatrice.

From: Beatrice Jones-Martin
To: Isabel Jones
15 September, 2004, 01:50 p.m.
Subject: He is back with her

Dear Isabel,

I'd love to speak with you, but I think that all I'll do is crumble in tears. So here is a copy of the mail I have sent to Paul. If the children were not here, I would have left Edward a long time ago. I feel so trapped. Speak to you soon.

X
B

From: Isabel Jones
To: Beatrice Jones-Martin
15 September, 2004, 10:05 p.m.
Subject: He is back with her

I'm sorry I missed your call tonight, I was cooking. I am outraged and really heart-broken for you. I can feel your pain. But you know what, you are not trapped. You are a strong and clever woman. You can escape from this this man. I know he is my brother-in -law, but boy, what a jerk! He needs more than therapy, he needs a brain and a heart transplant. I'm sorry if my words are not comforting but I am so angry and wished I had some power to make things better for you Beatrice, and the children.

All I can say it that I ma here for you, to scream, to cry, to talk, to laugh, to do whatever you need; I'm here.

Love
Isabel

20

When you go

Edward returned home from work with a letter for me in his hand; he gave it to me saying that it was a song by Sinatra he'd heard a long time ago and it came to his mind today:

> When you go away on this summer day,
> Then you might as well take the sun away;
> All the birds that flew in the summer sky,
> When our love was new and our hearts were high;
> When the day was young and the night was long,
> And the moon stood still for the night bird's song.
> When you go away, when you go away, when you go away.

He had also written a letter at the back of the song, I sat down to read it:

Dear Beatrice,

I do not know what I was doing. My arrogance and usual flamboyant ways thought I could handle everything. Now I realise what an idot I was. This is what years of depression have done to me Beatrice, please believe me.

I am feeling better now, I am no longer under her spell, I can control myself and I wanted to be sure of that: My urges are gone.

I can see now how depressed you have become, like me. But together, we can repair all this damage. I need you by my side Beatrice, to rebuild and get through this small hurdle.

I need you Beatrice to heal.

As I finished reading this letter, I caught a glimpse of a red pen lying on the table. I picked it up and circled the words "my urges" and "small hurdle" with question marks next to them. What was I fighting against? My husband's urges for a 17-year-old? A "small" fucking "hurdle"? When did suicide attempts become "small hurdles"?

From: Beatrice Jones-Martin
To: Isabel Jones
15 September, 2004, 10:16 p.m.
Subject: He is back with her

He is at his therapist right now, but it's only the fourth session. Not much hope. There is no way that I can understand what's going on ... It is so unbelievable! He thought it would be okay, I did not know, yes another secret ... How many more? I really must go, but how can I do that to the kids? I cannot control the way that he feels for this little slut (excuse my language). He had to see her again! When is it going to end? Probably never, so I just have to face that, take my kids under my arms and go! Leave them two to enjoy themselves!

From: Isabel Jones
To: Beatrice Jones-Martin
15 September, 2004, 10:20 p.m.
Subject: He is back with her

This is quite chocking. Edward is an idiot and you'll do yourself a favor by leaving him. Stuff the promise to God, He'll understand, I'm sure. Edward had all a man could wish to have: a beautiful loving wife, with amazing children in a caring home.

We adore you all but it's time for you to escape this destructive relationship. Remember that I'll always be there for you and the children, even if we are far apart. Paul is mad at him but that will not change anything.

With love, Isabel X

From: Beatrice Jones-Martin
To: Isabel Jones
15 September 2004, 11:24 p.m.
Subject: Future? What future?

Well, apparently, going back with the slut is his way of attacking me because he is jealous of me. I know that because this afternoon, I took a walk to the psy and met him. I needed to speak to someone who had the ability to get into his mind and explain it to me. It's nothing else, according to his psy. Also, his self-esteem is so low that he thinks he does not deserve anything good in his life and feel better in creating miserable situations for himself. He does not think he is worthy of my love, so it's better to destroy it.

Does this make sense to you? I'm not a psy. He is trying to trick me once more, isn't he? He is out to destroy what is good because he only sees himself as bad?

Whatever happens, you must know that I love you all very much and I would never deprive my children from being in touch with all their cousins and you. It's too important to their well-being!

I do not know what to do … It might be best to stop and think and organise my life differently. I will phone his psy to meet him. For someone has to give me a rational explanation for this.

Thank you for all your support, Isabel. The distance is nothing … Don't worry about it. I'll go to bed now and will talk to you tomorrow.

Love u lots,
B.

21

The show must go on

Every morning, I got up, got ready, and went to work. He did the same, our children did the same, our au pair did the same. We have become like robots who think too much but are trapped in our environment, too scared to change it, too scared to run away from it. The thoughts eat you slowly but surely and you do not know where to turn for help. Following that night, I wanted to talk to Pearl, or to my mother, but the shame and embarrassment would stop me, whispering 'the show must go on'.

I really felt as though I was on a stage, a very bad play was put together, and all the audience was laughing at me, not with me. I wanted to escape from the stage, to return to my reality, but I could not, the show had to go on.

With suspicion back on my mind, the best times of the day were in class, in front of my students. There I could not think of anything else but teach them. However, as soon as I left the class, thoughts of the slut and Edward came back hitting my head with an invisible but powerful hammer. Are they somewhere together? Is he on the phone with her? Has he sent her an e-mail from school? How do I know what he's up to? Are they meeting in another restaurant? At my house? Are they fucking in a dark alley somewhere dirty? Are they trying to make love in a public toilet? So far, I had been completely naive and so wrong. I never saw them coming. I wished I could wake up from this living nightmare, run away from this bad play, and escape from my robotic, stupid life. I could not. I was no longer in control of my life, the only thing that mattered was that the show went on. Must save what was left, even though it was painful. I just did not know what was left exactly. I was lost.

22

The theatre tickets

Tuesday
21 09 04

Yet another uneventful day in school and a long meeting to close it off. I left the main block at about 07:00 p.m. to go to the other site car park. The lane leading to the other school site always scares me at night when I leave late from meetings. I ran straight ahead to the lit part of the road and crossed over to get into my car. I was so tired, but I ignored the car and returned to my office to pick up a few more piles of documents to read, that I would probably not read.

It was almost 07:45 p.m. when I opened my boot to throw that bloody heavy leather bag of mine, full of work papers and books, just for the fun of it. Unfortunately, my eyes stopped on a silver envelop which lay there at the edge of the boot. I picked it up. It was empty, but just underneath it, two tickets had slipped. I picked them up. I nearly screamed when I read 'Student A Mainyu' on the booking reference line. They were theatre tickets for a play at the Globe Theater on Saturday, 10 July 07:30 p.m.: The Taming of the Shrew. 'She had been in my car, again!' I screamed out loud in the dark empty car park. She had bought some theatre tickets for them. Who the hell does she think she is? Is she ever going to go away! How the fuck did those tickets end up in my car? Why were they there? Who put them there? Edward had the car yesterday, did he see her yesterday again? I picked up the silver envelop again and 'Edward' was written on the front. It's a birthday card envelop, where is the card she wrote? I frantically searched through the mess of Edward's old displays scattered on the boot floor. Nowhere, no birthday card. Tenth of July? Edward was still in hospital, so they could not have gone. She was planning to take him out in the evening, probably for his birthday, but that never happened … My hands were shaking, but my mind kept throbbing with questions and suppositions.

I threw the tickets on the front seat and sat down to drive, in a rage. How the fuck did those tickets end up in my car, with her name on them? She had to give me an explanation. She had to give me a long bloody fucking explanation! I've had enough of that little fucking slut. I'm losing it! I set up my mobile phone on hands free, nearly ran over an old lady that I did not see on the yellow crossing; the motorcyclist behind me gave me an earful of swear words when he saw that I had been fiddling with my mobile phone.

'Hello?' a young voice replied.

'Hello, Ariana, it's Beatrice Jones-Martin, can you …' She put the phone down before I finished my question. I laughed nervously, but also amused as she was obviously scared of me. She had to be, I had given her enough warnings to stop fooling around with my husband. If she'd put the phone down so abruptly, she certainly knew that she was in the wrong, not wanting to face me again.

I dialled the number again and again while driving back home. She never answered and each time her voicemail would repeat: 'This is the Virgin voicemail for Ariana, please leave a message,' so I left many messages, each of them saying: 'Ariana, we have to talk.' She never answered, we never spoke. I rang all evening. The next day, I called again, I became obsessed, furious, I had to talk to her. During the day, I rang, after school, I rang, but each and every time, the voicemail spoke to me instead of her, making me even more obsessive and blind to my anger. I tried for two days. How no one noticed my rage at work, I did well to hide it, I had to. Edward did not know what was happening, no one knew about the inner torture I was going through. If I had told him, he would have tried to protect her. The irony was that I, too, was trying to protect her.

The initial anger from finding the theatre tickets turned into anxiety for Edward's state of mind. Every morning in the car, he was telling me how 'bad' he was 'feeling, worth than on June 21st'. He was talking about 'constant nightmares and being scared of the dark'. Edward seemed so lost and helpless at times, I had to speak to her. It might become dangerous for her to meet with him. He was suicidal again. What if he decided to drive her somewhere and kill her before killing himself? The desperate suicidal scenario floated in my head for a few days.

Edward had become impossible to please and he was sucking out all of my energy with anxiety and panic attacks. I had to speak to her. She had to know about the real Edward, she had to get away from him. He was suicidal, totally unstable. She had to know. I contaminated myself with the idea of warning her whilst hating her.

I got nowhere with the virgin voicemail and eased off the calls, but on the third day, frustration was overwhelming, and in a last attempt to speak with her, my message said, 'If you refuse to talk over the phone, I'll have to come and meet you in Shallow Lane, that's not difficult, is it?' I was imagining myself waiting for her to come home and calling her whilst standing by my car, to discuss outside her home. What was I thinking of? As if that would go very smoothly.

This is true that I am extremely naive, Edward had always said so. Anyhow, I waited for her to ring me back, but she never did. At least, she knew that I knew where she lived and maybe that would make her stop seeing my husband. So many thoughts went through my mind, but I could not help feeling that maybe that last message had been the wrong move.

23

Open Evening, open heart at school

Tuesday
28.09.04

Caring High School is packed, visitors eager to find out if we are suitable for their most cherished possession: their sons and daughters now in year 5 or year 6, about to start secondary school. All day, teachers had been working so hard to make the school look its best: displays renewed, environment cleaned, checked, and rechecked.

There is tension, but also excitement, a big show is about to take place, and I'm a main actress in it: I welcome the visitors in the foyer. Big voice, big smile, perfect discreet makeup, French accent, impeccable suit, got to look the part: welcoming and business-like. Tonight, I can forget about my tormented home life and pretend to be happy, especially when our new colleague, Lawrence, stares at me from head to toe with his big brown eyes.

Lawrence Jackson started at Caring High School in April but was interviewed last December. Lawrence is extremely attractive. He is tall, black, very dark and mysterious, and I could guess the tight muscular chest underneath his shirt. The truth is, on his interview day, whilst giving him a tour of the school, I could not look at him in the eyes, he confused me with some unusual feelings I could not describe. He was so smart and elegant, walking along the school corridor like an actor receiving an ovation. Lawrence was undoubtedly charming and all the female staff in the library opened their mouth quite wide, Ally McBeal wide open style, as he entered a little late for his interview. He made an unforgettable entrance, we all agreed.

A few months after his appointment, the senior team had had the usual team building weekend away, and he had been invited, even though he had not officially started. He was effortlessly eloquent and convincing, quite astonishing indeed. I kept my distance and let Pearl get friendlier with him. We barely spoke to each other, I could not, I felt all nervous around him, but determined not to show it, so I kept my distance. This dark and gorgeous man had some intriguing effects on me.

The night of the open evening, we worked in perfect partnership to welcome parents. At times, above the crowd, I could sense his eyes touching me warmly, and it felt really special. I think I felt desire from Lawrence's dark and troubling gaze on me. Was I wrong? What was he thinking of? What if he simply had a genuine interest in me as a new colleague? I must be completely ridiculous, but those eyes … For the first time that night, at home, in bed, I was thinking about another man. I was eager for the morning to come to go to work and find out if I had been imagining those big brown eyes staring at the curves of my little body.

Lawrence's voice surprised me as I entered the staffroom the next morning. He was by his tray and asked me how I was since the night before. I replied shyly, 'Very well, thank you, and you?'

'Better for seeing you' was his response. No other colleague had ever said this to me before.

I was being a very silly woman, fantasising on her new colleague because her marriage was crumbling down. Had to gather my thoughts again and fight this urge to touch him, to get closer to his chest, to feel his hot skin, and to breathe in his scent. What was happening to me?

24

The shop is just round the corner

Thursday
30.09.04
09:00 p.m.

Edward went out to buy some Kaliber. Since June, he has been on a new drink regime: no alcohol. I remembered how we used to drink during our recovery period after April. We used to go to Bellavista Street trendy bars and order the most gigantic cocktails. One of them was called 'Cosmic Orgasm', which Edward would order as I would be too embarrassed to ask the male waiters, 'Can I have a Cosmic Orgasm please?'

One night, Edward disappeared from the bar for two minutes. When he returned, he had a pack of Silk Cut in his hand and a box of matches. I had not smoked since university in 1990s! I was so happy at the sight of the cigarettes, I smoke at least three in a row very slowly, I was in heaven again.

Edward was amazed. In our nine years of marriage, he had never seen me smoke and loved it. I was 'so different, so sexy' in his eyes. Suddenly, I had become the wild and naughty Beatrice that I used to be, many years ago. That night at the bar was fun and we had both felt free for a while: free from the reality that had brought us to go out one evening in the middle of the week: a special effort to try and save our marriage.

But tonight, he was going out late to get some Kaliber. A strange feeling of anxiety took over me as he closed the door. I ran upstairs to tell Rose that I was going out too to get something at the corner shop. I went out to follow Edward. I arrived in the shop but could not see him, so I went out. There he was, ahead of me, walking away towards home quite happily with a blue plastic bag in his hand. I was relieved until he suddenly stopped and turned towards the phone box just before crossing the road to go home.

I stopped too, stood on the pavement for one second listening to my heart banging its way out my chest. My breathing became faster and faster, my body started to sweat with cold. I moved closer to the phone box and hit its glass window. He startled with panic and fear all at once, all over his face.

'Who are you phoning?' I screamed.

'Err, err, Paul,' he mumbled painfully.

'Paul? From a phone box? Why not phone him at home? Stop lying to me Edward, you are phoning her!' I did not shout but yelled at him in the street.

'She is not answering her phone, I don't know why. She is not answering.' He was nearly crying but then realised what he had said and added, 'I just wanted to talk to her.'

'Why? Why do you keep hurting me? Why?' and I walked away, crossed the road. He ran after me and grabbed my wrist begging me with 'Sorry, sorry, it will not happen again, promise, I promise.' But I was too angry to respond and arguing in the street was not my style.

He started to scream: 'Please Beatrice, it's nothing!' He knew that he would get my attention by being loud because I would want to avoid alerting the neighbours with our marital argument in the street at 09:20 p.m.! I told him to calm down, that we would talk on the next day. If I had told him in the street that I really wanted to leave him, it would have been a nuclear catastrophe response from him, so I decided to play it down. What did I have to lose? We continued to walk home with Edward squeezing my hand and mumbling to himself, 'I will not let you leave me, I will not let you leave me, she is nothing, she is nothing, I only wanted to talk. I will kill myself if you leave me.' I did not answer.

As we arrived at the front door, he released me, but I did not enter the house straight away. I crossed the road to the other phone box opposite our lounge window and dialled her number, one last time. She did not answer, so I left one ultimate message: 'Ariana, I know that Edward has been trying to contact you. If you respond to his calls, you will lead him to suicide because he is mentally ill. If something happens to Edward, I will press charges against you for taking advantage of a mentally ill person.' I put the phone down and went home.

I found him in the kitchen, his head in his hand, sobbing. It was now the time to tell him why she was not answering her phone. He kept shaking his head. 'I had told you not to call her, I had told you not to call her.'

'What else was I supposed to do when I found those tickets in my car? Take them to the police, maybe?' I shouted, but not too loud as I did not want the children nor Rose to hear us. 'You should not have phoned her, Beatrice, she is nasty. You should not have phoned her, but you never listen to me.' He looked worried and was becoming very agitated. He started pacing the kitchen floor, the breakfast room, up and down, mumbling to himself, holding his head in his palms. Edward was now scaring me, he was acting the 'mad man', was he really going mad, totally irrational? Or was he acting it out?

He left the kitchen and went into the dining room, still mumbling, but now also hitting his head with his fists. I watched him from the doorway and told him to sit down, to stop 'pretending', but he ignored me. He eventually sat down but was so tense and agitated that I ran back to the kitchen to pick up the phone. Next to him, I asked him to dial the Samaritans, which he did. This time, he cried throughout the conversation with a lady at the other end of the line. He was so helpless, I felt so hopeless. What was happening to us? What was happening to our lives? Could we not have stopped before falling down so low? I was very scared for our future, I could not see it, I had lost sight of it.

The Samaritan lady was listening carefully to him and I guessed that was all he needed for the moment. He cried as he told his story of lies and deception, of suicidal thoughts, and loss of hope. My body froze as I knelt down next to him and laid my cheek on his lap, trying to comfort him, or myself? Edward returned to a normal state as he put the phone down. We did not talk to each other; there was nothing more to say, it was very late.

25

They came

Monday
04-10-04

Today, I decided to have my hair back in a tight ponytail, maybe a last attempt to push all the problems back and keep them firmly held behind my neck. The dress I wore was not Edward's favourite, he usually compared it to 'a sack', it did not matter, I liked it: long, straight, simple, and black linen, no fancy tricks about it. I put on my passion pink cardigan to enhance the dress, the tall black boots, and I left to go to work. I felt fine actually, considering the trauma of last Thursday.

From my office window, I could see the top of the trees swaying in the early morning wind. There is no one in the car park, just my car and that silver people carrier who looked like it had gone into the wrong entrance. The driver came out: a ginger-headed man with broad shoulders. He seemed lost. He moved forward to talk to someone over the fence of the kinder garden, obviously asking for directions. His car was filled with other people. He turned back and disappeared down the road.

I carried on with my makeup, the feel-good factor thing I do every morning in my office, before switching on the computer. It was like a ritual, and if I was too late to do it, I knew I would have a bad day. Not for failing to fulfil my vanity, which was partly true, but for not taking time for myself. Once I left the office to go to staff briefing, that would be it, I would not have one second to think about me, except when I had to squeeze my legs tightly to remind me that I could not go to the toilets in the middle of teaching. I had just about finished with the burgundy lip gloss when the phone rang. Who's bloody calling me so early? It's not 08:00 a.m. yet.

'Hi, Beatrice, there's a gentleman here from the police asking for you.' I recognise Kate's voice from the school office, and ask her: 'Me? Are you sure?'

'Yes, he asked for you by name.'

'Okay, say I'm on my way,' and I put the phone down. I grab my beige coat, forget the scarf, and I leave my office.

Have they found Edward dead somewhere? After last night, what did he do this morning? Why is the police here, asking for me 'by name', what do they want? Where is Edward? I arrived to the school reception and entered the waiting room. Four tall, stern-looking people are there, waiting for me. One of them starts straightaway: 'Are you Beatrice Jones-Martin?' her voice is deep and husky. I'm surprised by it. 'Yes, that's me.'

'Do you know Ariana Mainyul?' she asked with a very poignant look in her eyes, almost hatred. When she mentioned that name, I felt fear climbing up my spine. Fear for me, fear for Edward. I muttered, 'Yes, well, I know of her.'

'Well, you are under arrest for harassment against her with threat to kill.'

'What? I never ...' I screamed and fell back on the seat behind me.

'Do not say anything that could be used against you' etc. etc. I am no longer listening, I am gone, I cannot believe this is happening to me, today, in school. 'You have to follow us now to your house for a search' the husky voice continued to husk in my ear.

'But I need to inform my head and get my bag from my office.' As I said that, they all looked at each other as though trying to work out if I could be trusted not to run away or kill myself on the spot. 'Where's the head office?' the ginger head asked.

'Just over there,' I said pointing towards the outside staircase, but as I went the back way instead to access the head's office, they all followed me in silence. Passed the bursar's office and asked if the head was around, negative answer. Asked his PA, negative answer. Maurice was nowhere to be found. He is always in his office at that time in the morning before briefing. Why isn't he here today? Did he know they were coming and hid himself somewhere? I need to talk to him. I need to see him. He will tell them that they are making a mistake, that I have classes to teach, I can't just leave them and go. Where is he? Why isn't he here today? I resign myself to ask the four robots to give me time to write a note on his desk. Ginger Hair nods.

Dear Maurice,

I have to leave school now (8:15). The police want to interview me about my husband and the girl. I will call you later. Beatrice.

Why did I lie on my note? Why couldn't I write that the police is arresting me for harassing the slut who was giving blow jobs to my husband? I was too ashamed. I could not possibly say those words, and writing them would have engraved them in his memory and mine forever, so I chose to pretend. After all, I was going to be interviewed, but not exactly as a witness, I was a suspect. Ginger Hair read the note before leaving the head's office and they all followed me back to my tree top office.

We left from the back door to walk up the narrow road which led to the other car park. I never realised how long that narrow road was before. Two officers walked in front of me and two walked behind me. The students were walking to school, happy and greeting me with bright smiles and 'Hello Miss!' I could barely look at them in the eyes to reply. I wondered if they knew that they were arresting me, that these robots were not parents, that they were not teachers. They were arresting me. Luckily, they were not in uniform, but they looked very serious, serious enough for a few teachers to frown at their sight with me, as we walked in opposite directions.

Their intrigued look tells me that they can sense my fear, but they say nothing and continued walking to school. I continued walking back towards my office with the four robots.

In the office, I searched for a few things: my mobile, my diary, a pen, and threw the lot in my bag. I considered for one minute to dig out the secret e-mails I was keeping in the inside zip pocket of my school bag, that would prove that I am innocent, that the slut is to blame, not me! I decided to leave them in the bag. They are my divorce evidence and I do not actually know how the police would see all those. I left them there. The robots did not notice me staring at the satchel; they just stood there till we left my office.

Back in the car park, their car was missing. I noticed then that only three robots were with me, the fourth one was probably in the car. We crossed the car park, again, and the road. I did not look and I would have been hit by the coming car onto my right if Ginger Hair had not put his strong arm in front of me to stop me from walking into a speedy car. The driver's honking woke me up from my suicidal glazed walk. At the end of the narrow road, the police car was waiting, its engine running. The two female officers sat in the back with me and Ginger Hair sat in the front passenger seat near Tall Skinny guy driving.

They headed towards my home, why? 'We have to search your house, we went this morning at seven-thirty but you had left already and your au pair did not understand who we were.' I could not believe what I heard. Searching my house, for what? A gun? Drugs? Who do they think I am? Don't they have other criminals to chase? At least I am in a civilian's car, the shame would have been too unbearable had I been in a police car. What story or excuse would have explained my presence in a police car outside my front door, other than I am a criminal or a would-be criminal.

As I opened the door, Rose was standing in the hallway looking very worried, she did not speak to me, but the look in her eyes was desperately questioning me. The police guys spread around the house, they found my old laptop in the dining room and took it with them in a clear plastic bag.

Upstairs, in Julien's room, Ginger Hair commented on the nice decor and asked me about the white furniture. I replied that it was from Ikea, but wondered why was he trying to be 'nice'? I did not even know his name. They went into all the rooms, and as I tried to speak in French with Rose, Ginger Hair raised his hand to stop me in my sentence. I stared at him and said, 'My au pair is really worried and I need to tell her to take care of the children till I return, I cannot tell her that in English.'

He nodded and I told Rose, 'Edward et moi, on vient d'être arrêtés à cause d'allégations d'une de ses élèves, tu dois t'occuper des enfants jusqu'à mon retour. Ne t'inquiète pas, je rentre ce soir.'[3] Rose acknowledged my instructions without a word, nodding her head nervously; she looked so terrified, but there was nothing I could do to change that anxious feeling.

After a round which revealed nothing from my house, Ginger Hair declared that we had to go to the station for questioning. He went towards the front door, I followed him, crossed the road and entered the silver car

---

[3] "Edward and I have just been arrested because of the allegations of one of his students, you must take care of the children until I come back home. Don't worry, I'll be back tonight."

where Husky Voice and her colleague had been waiting. I was told to sit in the back, between the two female officers.

Where were they taking me? To Crawley police station, in Surrey. The ride from my house to the station was long and painfully silent. My mind was retracing the phone calls I had made, the conversations I had had when I met the slut, the conversations I had tried to have. She had actually never spoken to me after the theatre tickets, how could I be accused of making 'threats to kill?' What about her involvement with my husband? I was trying to save my marriage! I thought of the arguments with Edward, the mysteries, the suicide attempt, the coma, the hospital white corridor … And now, I was in a police car driving me to a station to be interrogated like a criminal. I never saw that coming.

Happiness is a dark stale illusion.

26

The end

It was 10:00 a.m. when we arrived in the station. A very small entrance from the car park led to a reception with a very tall desk. The police officer perched behind, looked down at me, and asked me to confirm my identity. I said my name, I could barely hear my own voice, I was shaking. She asked for my nationality too. I told her I was French. She replied that the French authority will be informed of my arrest as a French national. She then read very quickly what I was accused of. I retained very little, she spoke too fast. She mentioned 'repeated threats to kill Ariana Mainyul, phone calls, harassment'. I started to panic inside, but kept calm. Suddenly, I heard a voice shouting at the end of the corridor, it sounded like Edward!

'Is my husband here?' I asked, anxious to find myself near him.

'Yes, he was arrested too this morning,' the officer said in a very stern voice, no smile, no emotions. I felt cold suddenly. I asked for a copy of the document she read, she refused to give it to me and asked if I wanted to call someone.

I looked for my mobile in my handbag and searched for Jane's number. The officer instructed me to use the police phone on the high desk. I dialled her number.

'Jane, it's Beatrice, I've been arrested by the police because of your brother's affair with his student. I'm going to fucking divorce him. Please find me a lawyer, Jane. I'm in Crawley police station.'

'What? Oh my God. Where is Edward?' She asked breathless.

'He's been arrested too, he's here but I can't see him.'

'You only have five minutes for your call' the officer blurted out.

'Jane, please find me a lawyer.' I put the phone down.

Jane was the first person who came to my mind, so I called her. I really felt lonely like an orphan, no family to support me, my family was in Paris, unaware of the crisis I was going through. Calling Jane was the closest I could get to family.

The female officer behind the tall desk blew away my thoughts by telling me to follow her colleague for my photograph to be taken, but I had to leave all my belongings with her first. I had to remove everything. My handbag, my mobile, my necklace, my bracelets, my rings, my watch, all went into a clear plastic bag with my name and date on the label. I asked to keep my watch, it was 10:20 a.m. She agreed without talking.

I followed her colleague to a small room near the reception. There she placed me in front of a white wall, took out an enormous camera, and took a picture of me. She then explained about my fingerprints being taken too. I moved to a table nearby the wall, and as she held the top of my hand, she pushed each individual finger into the ink pad before placing them on a special card, one by one. This was horrible because it was not a fiction police series I was watching on TV. This was real, happening to me, like a criminal. My fingerprints, my photo were going to be on record, nationally or internationally, I did not know. And as the fingerprints were taken from both hands, she faced me and grabbed some elongated cotton buds from a shelf next to the fingerprints table. She told me that my DNA sample had to be taken. I had to open my mouth. I did, and she swiped that long cotton bud against my cheeks, my gum. She took another one and repeated the process, going thoroughly inside my mouth, before inserting them into some clear tubes. When she finished, I lowered my head and could feel a tear running down my face. I wiped it quickly. Was this a tear for fear, for shock, for anger? I did not know. I was no longer in control of anything; my thoughts, my body were no longer mine. They belonged to the police.

We left the small office and returned near the tall reception desk. I followed the DNA officer, who then left me there to go further into the corridor. The desk female officer asked me, 'Do you have a solicitor?'

'No, I don't. I've asked my sister-in-law to send me one,' I replied, thinking that this would be unlikely to happen, Jane was just too far up North!

'Do you want an assigned solicitor?'

'Yes, please.'

'Okay, we'll get you a solicitor on duty. Jim, take her to her cell!' She shouted at the male officer who had appeared behind me.

A cell? Now? Like a prisoner? This did not make any sense to me. I had contacted the slut, tried to save my marriage, tried to keep her away from suicidal Edward, and I was arrested, Edward was arrested. She had obviously turned against him now, against both of us. Where was he taking me?

The walk to the cell led us to a long corridor where large royal blue metallic doors with bars at the top were spread on each side. They were the doors to the cells. The male officer opened the last door on the corridor saying, 'There you are.' I entered and he closed the royal blue door behind me with a big metallic bang, I heard his keys turning twice in the locks. I slowly turned round to look. My tears endlessly ran down my face, my neck, and wet the top of my black dress, I could not stop them. The whole morning arrest was suddenly hitting me with a big and heavy invisible weapon I could not see, but could only feel down my stressed throat and eyes. I wanted to scream, but could not. It felt like a nightmare that was only starting; how worse could this be in comparison with the suicide attempt of June? Why was God punishing me this way? Had I not kept my promise, despite all the hurt and pain? I never saw you coming, Edward.

TO BE CONTINUED IN…

NOW, LIVE WITH THAT!

by

KLS Fuerte